"A Prince With Benefits. That Does Sound Intriguing."

She tapped her chin and pretended to think.

Adan had resisted her long enough—his last thought before he reeled her into his arms and kissed her. Piper didn't reject the gesture at all. She didn't push him away or tense against him. She simply kissed him back like a woman who had not been kissed enough.

Bent on telling her what she was doing to him, he brought his lips to her ear. "If we had no care in the world, and all the privacy we needed, I would lift up your dress, lower your panties and take you right here."

She pulled back and stared at him with hazy eyes. "I could think of worse things."

He could think of something much better. "You deserve a bed and champagne and candles our first time."

"You're certainly not lacking in confidence."

Subtlety had never been his strongest suit. "Provided we decide to take that next step."

"Provided we could actually find the time to do it while adhering to your son's schedule."

Right on time, the sound of a crying baby filtered out through the nursery's open window.

* * *

The Sheikh's Son is part of the #1 bestselling miniseries from Harlequin Desire—Billionaires and Babies: Powerful men...wrapped around their babies' little fingers.

* * *

If you're on Twitter,
tell us what you think of Harlequin Desire!
#harlequindesire

Dear Reader,

If you're a romantic at heart, you know the fantasy. You've probably heard the setup in a song or two. You see a handsome stranger seated across the room. He gives you more than a passing glance. A conversation ensues, and you assume this chance encounter will only last one night. Dare you hope it could last a lifetime? Probably not, but that doesn't stop you from wishing the fantasy might lead to a future. Maybe you'll be one of those lucky couples that meet and marry ten days later, and stay married at least fifty years. Hey, it happens.

Of course, you have to worry that the gorgeous man occupying your time isn't all he claims to be, even if he is the consummate charmer. And he has to-die-for dimples. But you also sense he has secrets. Major secrets. Heaven forbid if you learn a few other things he failed to mention, like he's not only a pilot, but an Arabian prince. Of course, there is that baby issue, and as everyone knows, a baby changes everything.

That scenario might sound implausible, but when it comes to a love story—or love in general—anything is possible. And the whole "strangers in the night" fantasy is the basis for this book featuring Adan, the youngest son of the royal Mehdi family, who meets his match in Piper McAdams. He's a sexy devil who's determined to prove he's honorable. She's a natural beauty with a nurturing soul. Neither have lofty relationship expectations, but they certainly can't ignore chemistry, or the emotional connection that develops as a result.

I truly hope you enjoy tracking Adan and Piper's journey as much as I enjoyed writing it. But hang on to your book—it's going to be a bumpy ride.

Happy reading!

Kristi

THE SHEIKH'S SON

—

KRISTI GOLD

Recycling programs
for this product may
not exist in your area.

ISBN-13: 978-0-373-73326-2

THE SHEIKH'S SON

Copyright © 2014 by Kristi Goldberg

Printed in U.S.A.

Books by Kristi Gold

Harlequin Desire

The Return of the Sheikh #2230
One Night with the Sheikh #2244
From Single Mom to Secret Heiress #2300
The Sheikh's Son #2313

Silhouette Desire

Marooned with a Millionaire #1517
Expecting the Sheikh's Baby #1531
Fit for a Sheikh #1576
Challenged by the Sheikh #1585
Persuading the Playboy King #1600
Unmasking the Maverick Prince #1606
Daring the Dynamic Sheikh #1612
Mistaken for a Mistress #1669
A Most Shocking Revelation #1695
House of Midnight Fantasies #1728
The Pregnancy Negotiation #1763
Executive Seduction #1768

Harlequin Superromance

His Best Mistake #1624
§*The One She Left Behind* #1732
§*The Son He Never Knew* #1744
§*The Only Man for Her* #1785

Harlequin Everlasting Love

Fall from Grace

Harlequin Special Edition

Through Jenna's Eyes #1836
The Mommy Makeover #1956

§Delta Secrets
*The Royal Wager

Other titles by this author
available in ebook format.

KRISTI GOLD

has a fondness for beaches, baseball and bridal reality shows. She firmly believes that love has remarkable healing powers and feels very fortunate to be able to weave stories of love and commitment. As a bestselling author, a National Readers' Choice Award winner and a Romance Writers of America three-time RITA® Award finalist, Kristi has learned that although accolades are wonderful, the most cherished rewards come from networking with readers. She can be reached through her website, at www.kristigold.com, or through Facebook.

To Bob...for giving me a quiet place to finish this book, and for showing me that new beginnings do happen when least expected.

One

If a woman wanted a trip to paradise, the gorgeous guy seated at the bar could be just the ticket. And Piper McAdams was more than ready to board that pleasure train.

For the past twenty minutes, she'd been sitting at a corner table in the Chicago hotel lounge, nursing a cosmopolitan while shamelessly studying the stranger's assets, at least those she could readily see in the dim light. He wore an expensive silk navy suit, a pricey watch on his wrist and his good looks like a badge of honor. His dark brown hair seemed as if it had been intentionally cut in a reckless—albeit sexy—style, but it definitely complemented the slight shading of whiskers framing his mouth. And those dimples. She'd spotted them the first time he smiled. Nothing better than prominent dimples on a man, except maybe…

The questionable thought vaulted into Piper's brain like a bullet, prompting her to close her eyes and rub her temples as if she had a tremendous headache. She chalked up the reaction to her long-standing membership in the Unintentional Celibacy Club. She wasn't necessarily a prude, only picky. She certainly wasn't opposed to taking sex out for a spin before saying, "I do," in the context of a committed relationship. She simply hadn't found the right man, though not from the lack of trying. But never, ever in twenty-six years had she considered ending her sexual drought with a complete stranger…until tonight.

The sound of laughter drew her gaze back to said stranger, where the pretty blond bartender leaned toward him, exposing enough cleavage to rival the Grand Canyon. Oddly, he continued to focus on Blondie's face, until his attention drifted in Piper's direction.

The moment Piper met his gaze and he grinned, she immediately glanced back to search for a bathroom or another blonde but didn't find either one. When she regarded him again and found his focus still leveled on her, she started fiddling with her cell phone, pretending to read a nonexistent text.

Great. Just great. He'd caught her staring like a schoolgirl, and she'd just provided a big boost to his ego. He wouldn't be interested in her, a nondescript, ridiculously average brunette, when he had a tall, well-endowed bombshell at his disposal. He could probably have any willing woman within a thousand-mile radius, and she wouldn't be even a blip on his masculine radar. She took the mirror out of her purse and did a quick check anyway, making sure her bangs were smooth and her mascara hadn't gone askew beneath her eyes.

And going to any trouble for a man like him was simply ridiculous. History had taught her that she more or less attracted guys who found her good breeding and trust fund extremely appealing. Nope, Mr. Hunky Stranger would never give her a second look....

"Are you waiting for someone?"

Piper's heart lurched at the sound of his voice. A very deep, and very British, voice. After she'd recovered enough to sneak a peek, her pulse started to sprint again as she came up close and personal with his incredible eyes. Eyes that were just this shade of brown and remarkably as clear as polished topaz. "Actually, no, I'm not waiting for anyone," she finally managed to say in a tone that sounded as if she was playing the frog to his prince, not the other way around.

He rested his hand on the back of the opposing chair, a gold signet ring containing a single ruby circling his little finger. "Would you mind if I join you?"

Mind? Did birds molt? "Be my guest."

After setting his drink on the table, he draped his overcoat on the back of the chair, sat and leaned back as if nothing out of the ordinary had occurred. Then again, this was probably the norm for him—picking up someone in a bar. For Piper, not so much.

"I'm surprised you're not keeping company with a man," he said. "You are much too beautiful to spend Saturday night all alone."

She was surprised she hadn't fainted from the impact of his fully formed grin, the sexy half-moon crescent in his chin and the compliment. "Actually, I just left a cocktail party a little while ago."

He studied her curiously. "In the hotel?"

She took a quick sip of her drink and nearly tipped

the glass over when she set it down. "Yes. A party in honor of some obscenely rich sheikh from some obscure country. I faked a headache and left before I had to endure meeting him. That's probably a good thing, since for the life of me, I can't remember his name."

"Prince Mehdi?"

"That's it."

"I happened to have left there a few moments ago myself."

Lovely, Piper. Open mouth, insert stiletto. "Do you know the prince?"

"I've known him for a very long time. Since birth, actually." He topped off the comment with another slow smile.

She swallowed around her mortification while wishing for a giant crevice to open up and swallow her whole. "I'm sorry for insulting your friend. I just have an aversion to overly wealthy men. I've never found one who isn't completely consumed with a sense of entitlement."

He rimmed his finger around the edge of the clear glass. "Actually, some would say he's a rather nice fellow."

She highly doubted that. "Is that your opinion?"

"Yes. Of the three Mehdi brothers, he is probably the most grounded. Definitely the best looking of the whole lot."

When Piper suddenly realized she'd abandoned her manners, she held out her hand. "I'm Piper McAdams, and you are?"

"Charmed to meet you," he said as he accepted the handshake, and then slid his thumb over her wrist before letting her go.

She shivered slightly but recovered quickly. "Well, Mr. Charmed, do you have a first name?"

"A.J."

"No last name?"

"I'd like to preserve a little mystery for the time being. Besides, last names should not be important between friends."

Clearly he was hiding something, but her suspicious nature couldn't compete with her attraction to this mysterious stranger. "We're not exactly friends."

"I hope to remedy that before night's end."

Piper hoped she could survive sitting across from him without going into a feminine free fall. She crossed one leg over the other beneath the table and tugged at the hem of her cocktail dress. "What do you do for a living, A.J.?"

He loosened his tie before lacing his fingers together atop the table. "I am the personal pilot for a rich and somewhat notorious family. They prefer to maintain their privacy."

A pretty flyboy. Unbelievable. "That must be a huge responsibility."

"You have no idea," he said before clearing his throat. "What do you do for a living, Ms. McAdams?"

Nothing she cared to be doing. "Please, call me Piper. Let's just say I serve as a goodwill ambassador for clients associated with my grandfather's company. It requires quite a bit of travel and patience."

He inclined his head and studied her face as if searching for secrets. "McAdams is a Scottish name, and the hint of auburn in your hair and beautiful blue eyes could indicate that lineage. Yet your skin isn't fair."

She touched her cheek as if she had no idea she even

owned any skin. "My great-grandparents were Colombian on my mother's side. My father's family is Scottish through and through. I suppose you could say I'm a perfect mix of both cultures."

"Colombian and Scottish. A very attractive combination. Do you tan in the summer?"

A sudden image of sitting with him on a beach—sans swimwear—assaulted her. "I do when I find the time to actually go to the beach. I'm not home that often."

"And where is home?" he asked.

"South Carolina. Charleston, actually." She refused to reveal that she currently resided in the guesthouse behind her grandparents' Greek Revival mansion.

He hesitated a moment as if mulling over the information. "Yet you have no Southern accent."

"It disappeared when I attended an all-female boarding school on the East Coast."

He leaned forward with obvious interest. "Really? I attended military academy in England."

That certainly explained his accent. "How long were you there?"

His expression turned suddenly serious. "A bloody lot longer than I should have been."

She suspected a story existed behind his obvious disdain. "An all-male academy, I take it."

"Unfortunately, yes. However, the campus was situated not far from a parochial school populated with curious females. We were more than happy to answer that curiosity."

No real surprise there. "Did you lead the panty raids?"

His smile reappeared as bright as the illuminated beer sign over the bar. "I confess I attempted to raid a few panties in my youth, and received several slaps for my efforts."

She was consumed by pleasant shivers when she should be shocked. "I highly doubt that was always the case."

"Not always." He leaned back again, his grin expanding, his dimples deepening. "Did you fall victim to the questionable antics of boarding-school boys?"

She'd fallen victim to playing the wallflower, though she hadn't exactly been playing. "My school was located in a fairly remote area, and the rules were extremely strict. The headmistress would probably have shot first and asked questions later if a boy ever dared darken our doorstep."

His eyes held a hint of amusement. "I'm certain a woman with your looks had no difficulty making up for lost time once you escaped the confines of convention."

If he only knew how far off the mark he was with that assumption, he'd probably run for the nearest exit. "Let's just say I've had my share of boys darkening my doorstep. Most had last names for first names and more money than sexual prowess, thanks to my grandfather's insistence I marry within his social circles."

"Not a decent lover among them?"

Only one, and he'd been far from decent. She imagined A.J. would be a seriously good lover. She'd seriously like to find out. "Since I'm not into kissing and telling, let's move off that subject. Do you have a significant other?"

"I did have an 'other' almost a year ago, but she is no longer significant."

"Bad breakup?"

"Let's just say it took a while to convince her we did break up."

His sour tone told Piper that topic was also off-limits. On to more generic questions. "When I first spotted you at the bar, I was sure you're Italian. Am I right?"

Luckily his pleasant demeanor returned. "No, but I am quite fond of Italy, and I do know Italian, courtesy of a former teacher."

"My second guess would be you're of French descent."

"Je ne suis pas français, mais je peux bien embrasser à la francaise."

A sexy devil with devastating dimples and a wry sense of humor—a deadly combination. "I'm sure the parochial girls appreciated your French-kissing expertise. But you didn't exactly answer my question about your heritage."

"I am not of French, but I am impressed you speak the language."

She laid a dramatic palm over her breast and pulled out her best Southern speak. "Why, sugar, we're not all dumb belles. I know French and German and even a little Japanese."

"Should you find yourself in need of an Italian translator, I would be happy to accommodate you."

She would be thrilled if he did more than that. "I've never been to Italy but I've always wanted to see Rome."

"You should make that a priority. I personally prefer Naples and the coast...."

As he continued, Piper became completely mesmerized by his mouth, and began to ridiculously fantasize about kissing him. Then her fantasies took major flight as she entertained thoughts of his mouth moving down her body. Slow and warm and, oh, so…

"…large pink salmon walk down the streets texting on their smartphones."

She rejoined reality following the odd declaration. "I beg your pardon?"

"Clearly I bored you into a near coma while playing the travel guide."

He'd inadvertently drawn her into a waking sex dream. "I'm so sorry," she said. "It must be the booze."

He reached over and without an invitation took a drink from her glass, then set it down with a thud. "That is bloody awful," he said. "What is in this unpalatable concoction?"

Piper turned her attention to the drink and momentarily became preoccupied with the fact his lips had caressed the glass. And that was probably as close to his lips she would get…unless she took the plunge and turned the good girl to bad. "Basically vodka and cranberry juice, but the bartender made it fairly strong. It's gone straight to my head." And so had he.

He pushed his half-full glass toward her. "Try this."

She picked up the tumbler and studied the amber liquid. "What is it?"

"Twenty-year-old Scotch. Once you've sampled it, no other drink will do."

She would really like to sample him, and if she didn't stop those thoughts in their tracks, she might derail her common sense. "I'm not sure I should. I don't want to have to crawl to the hotel room."

"If you need assistance, I'll make certain you arrive safely."

Piper returned his wily smile. "Well, in that case, I suppose I could have a small sip."

The minute the straight liquor hit her throat, she truly wanted to spit it out. Instead, she swallowed hard and handed the tumbler back to him.

"You don't like it?" he asked, sounding somewhat insulted.

"Sorry, but it's just not my cup of tea. Or cup of alcohol, I should say. But then, I can't claim to have good drinking skills."

"How are your kissing skills?" Right when she was about to suggest they find out, he straightened, looked away and cleared his throat again. "My apologies. You are too nice a woman to endure my habit of spewing innuendo."

"Why do you believe I wouldn't appreciate a little harmless innuendo?"

He streaked a hand over his jaw. "You have a certain innocence about you. Perhaps even purity."

Here we go again.... "Looks can be deceiving."

"True, but eyes do not deceive. I've noticed your growing discomfort during the course of our conversation."

"Have you considered my discomfort stems from my attraction to you?" Heavens, she hadn't really just admitted that, had she? Yes, she had. Her gal pals would be so proud. Her grandfather would lock her up and toss away the key.

"I'm flattered," he said without taking his gaze from hers. "I must admit I find you very attractive as well, and I would like to know you better. Because of that, I have a request. You are under no obligation to agree, but I hope you will."

The moment of truth had arrived. Would she be willing to hurl caution to the wind and sleep with him? Would she really take that risk when she knew so little about him, including his last name? Oh, heck yeah. "Ask away."

When A.J. stood and offered his hand, her heart vaulted into her throat. She held her breath and waited for the ultimate proposition, the word *yes* lingering on her lips.

"Piper McAdams, would you do me the honor of taking a walk with me?"

Sheikh Adan Jamal Mehdi did not take women on long walks. He took them to bed. Or he had before he'd taken that bloody vow of celibacy eight months before in order to be taken more seriously by his brothers. A vow that had suddenly lost its appeal.

Yet Piper McAdams wasn't his usual conquest. She was witty and outgoing, while he normally attracted sophisticated and somewhat cynical women. She was only slightly over five feet tall, he would estimate, were it not for the four-inch heels, when he usually preferred someone closer in height to his six feet two inches. She also had surprisingly long legs and extremely full breasts for someone so small in stature, and he'd had trouble keeping his eyes off those assets for any length of time. The oath of restraint had not silenced his libido in any sense, especially now.

They strolled along the walkway bordering the lake for a good twenty minutes, speaking mostly in generalities, until Adan felt strangely at a loss for words. Conversation had always been his forte, and so had kissing.

He thought it best to concentrate on the first. "Do you have any siblings?"

When a gust of wind swirled around them, she pulled her hem-length black cashmere sweater closer to her body. "One. A twin sister whose official name is Sunshine, but she goes by Sunny, for obvious reasons."

He was immediately struck by the familiar name. "Sunny McAdams, the renowned journalist?"

Her smile showed a certain pride. "That would be her. We're actually fraternal twins, as if you couldn't figure that out from our obvious physical differences."

Yet neither woman lacked in beauty despite the fact one was blond and the other brunette. "Piper and Sunshine are both rather unusual names. Did they hold some significance for your parents?"

Her expression turned somber. "It's my understanding my mother named Sunny. Unfortunately, we don't know our father. Actually, we don't even know who he is, and I'm not sure my mother does, either. You could say we were a thorn in her socialite side. Our grandparents basically raised us for that reason."

That explained her sudden change in demeanor. But due to his own questions about his heritage, he believed discussing family dynamics in-depth should be avoided at all costs. "You said your mother named your sister. Who named you?"

"My grandfather did," she said with a smile. "He adores bagpipes."

Her elevated mood pleased him greatly. "I learned to play the bagpipes at school, but I quickly determined the kilts weren't at all my style."

She paused to lean back against the railing. "Tell

me something. Is it true that men wear nothing under those kilts?"

"A man needs some reminder that he is still a man while wearing a skirt." Being so close to this particular woman served to remind him of his manhood at every turn.

She laughed softly. "I suppose that's true. Why did your parents send you to boarding school?"

He'd asked that question many times, and he'd always received the same answer that he'd never quite believed. "I was an incorrigible lad, or so I'm told, and my father decided I could use the structure a military academy provides."

"Guess he wasn't counting on the panty raids."

Hearing the word *panty* coming out of her pretty mouth did not help his current predicament in the least. "He never learned about them as far as I know." His father had never really been close to his youngest son, if the truth were known.

"I'm sure if you'd ask him today," Piper said, "he'd probably admit he knew everything. Fathers and grandfathers have an uncanny knack of knowing your business."

He moved to her side, faced the lake and rested his hands on the railing. "My father passed away not long ago. My mother died some time ago."

"I'm sorry, A.J.," she said. "I didn't mean to be so thoughtless."

"No need to apologize, Piper. You had no way of knowing." Nor did she know he hailed from Middle Eastern royalty, and that bothered him quite a bit. Yet she had clearly stated she loathed men with fortunes, and he had a sizable one. For that reason, he would continue to keep that information concealed.

Tonight he preferred to be only the pilot, not the prince. "Did you attend university?" he asked, keeping his attention trained on the less-interesting view in order to keep his desire for her in check.

"Yes, I did. In South Carolina. An all-women's university. Evidently my grandfather believed I couldn't handle the opposite sex. But since he was footing the bill, I put up with it long enough to get the dreaded business degree."

He shifted to face her, one elbow braced on the top of the railing. "Since business is apparently not your chosen field of expertise, what would you do if you weren't playing the ambassador?"

"Art," she said without the slightest hesitation. "Painting is my passion."

He knew all about passion, only his involved planes. "Then why not pursue that dream?"

She sighed. "I have several reasons, most having to do with obligation."

"To your grandfather?"

"Yes."

Not so unlike his obligation to his legacy. "What about remaining true to yourself and your own happiness, Piper?"

A span of silence passed before she spoke again. "It's complicated."

Family dynamics always were, especially in his case.

When he noticed Piper appeared to be shivering, Adan cursed his thoughtlessness. "Obviously you're cold. Do you wish to return to the hotel now?"

She shook her head. "I'm fine. Really."

"You're wearing little more than a glorified sweater, and I suspect your teeth are chattering behind that beautiful mouth of yours."

Her laugh drew him further into her lair, as did the pleasant scent of her perfume. "Maybe a tad. It's rather nippy for April."

"Let me remedy that for you."

When Adan began to slip the buttons on his overcoat, Piper raised both hands as if to ward him off. "Heavens, no. I don't want to be responsible for you freezing to death."

Her smile alone generated enough heat in Adan to fuel half the city of Chicago. "Are you sure? I am accustomed to extreme temperatures."

"Seriously, I'm okay."

Without waiting for another protest, he shrugged out of his coat, wrapped it around her shoulders and took a step back. "Better?"

"Much better, but now you're going to be cold."

Not likely. Not while she stood before him with her dark hair blowing in the breeze, her bright blue eyes reflecting the light above them and her coral-painted lips enticing him to kiss her. Answering the invitation was a risk he didn't dare take.

She inhaled deeply then released a slightly broken breath. "I need something else from you, A.J."

He hoped she meant something warm to drink, a good excuse to retire back inside the hotel before he hurled wisdom to the blustery wind. "What would that be?"

"I need you to kiss me."

Bloody hell, what could he to say to that? Should he answer "absolutely not" when he wanted to blurt out a resounding yes? He brushed away a strand of hair from her cheek and ran his thumb along her jaw. "I'm not certain that would be a banner idea." Many times he had heard that phrase, but never coming out of his own mouth.

Disappointment called out from her eyes. "Why not?"

"Because if I kiss you, I would not want to stop with only a kiss."

She sent him an angel's smile. "Do you have issues with maintaining control?"

He prided himself on control when it came to flying jets and yes, wooing women. Still, there was something about this particular woman that told him he could end up losing the war he now waged with his libido.

Before he could respond, she wrapped her hand around his neck and lowered his lips to hers. He immediately discovered the angel kissed like the devil, and he liked it. He liked the way she tasted and the silken glide of her tongue against his, and he definitely liked the way she pressed her entire body against him. He would like it better if they were in his hotel bed without the hindrance of clothing. He did not particularly care for the warning bells sounding inside his brain.

Gathering every ounce of strength he still possessed, Adan pulled away and stepped back before he did something they might both regret. The dejected look on Piper's face gave him pause, and the urge to come up with some viable excuse. "You, lovely lady, are too much of a temptation for even the most controlled man."

Her expression brightened. "No one has ever accused me of that before."

"Apparently you have not been with anyone who appreciates your finer points."

Now she looked somewhat coy. "But you appreciate them?"

If she could see the evidence of his appreciation, she would not have posed the question. "I more than appreciate them, as I also appreciate and respect you. Therefore I am going to escort you back to the hotel and bid you good night." Or crush his determination to refrain from sex for three more months.

Piper pretended to pout. "But the night is still young, and I'm still cold."

"All the more reason to deliver you safely inside the hotel."

"Your room or mine?"

She seemed determined to make this incredibly hard on him…in every sense of the word. "Your room, and then I will retire to mine."

She sighed. "All right, if that's what you really want."

If he said that, he would be lying. "It's not a question of if I want you. The question is, would it be wise to continue this?"

"And your answer?"

"Completely unwise."

"Maybe we should ignore wisdom and do what comes naturally. We're both of age and free to do as we please, so why not take advantage of the opportunity?"

Just as he opened his mouth to issue another unenthusiastic argument, she kissed him again. Deeper this time, more insistent. He slid his hand down her back, cupped her bottom and brought her up against his erection, hoping to discourage her. The plan failed. She made a move with her hips and sent him so close to the edge that he considered lifting her skirt, lowering his pants and dispensing with all propriety.

The last thread of his coveted self-control prevented him from acting on his desire. He refused to succumb to animal instinct. He could not discard the vow, or his common sense, for one night of unbridled passion with someone he was clearly deceiving. He would remain strong, stay grounded, ignore the fact that he had a beautiful, sensual woman at his disposal and...

Whom was he attempting to fool? "Let's retire to my room."

Two

She had always strived to be the good twin. Straight as an arrow. Boring as hell. Never before had she demonstrated such assertiveness toward a man.

Now remarkably Piper found herself alone in an elevator with that man, with only one goal in mind—ending her self-imposed celibacy in a virtual stranger's hotel room. Oddly A.J. kept his distance and remained silent as they traveled all the way to the top floor. After the doors sighed open and they stepped out of the car, she expected to see a corridor containing a line of rooms. Instead she noticed only one double mahogany door flanked by two massive, stoic guards. If a pilot warranted this much security, then he must work for an incredibly powerful family or some high-ranking politician.

A.J. lightly clasped her elbow to guide her forward

before stopping at the entry to mutter something in what she assumed to be Arabic. One of the men turned immediately, slid a card key in the lock and opened the doors. As soon as they were safely sequestered inside, Piper took a moment to survey the area—exquisite dark wood floors, towering windows revealing the Chicago skyline, even a baby grand piano in the corner. An opulent penthouse designed for the rich and infamous. Her current companion was one lucky employee.

Piper started to comment on that very thing, but her words never made it to her open mouth. A.J. did, and the kiss he gave her had the impact of a firebomb. Somehow she ended up with her back against one wall with A.J. pressed against her, her face bracketed in his palms. When he shrugged the sweater from her shoulders, slipped it away and tossed it behind him, her heart rate began to run amok. Any concerns flittered away on the heels of a heat she'd never felt before with any man. But this man knew what he was doing, right down to the way he brushed kisses along the line of her jaw and her neck before he brought his mouth to her ear. "The bedroom," he whispered. "Now."

Okay, that would be the next step. A daring step. A step Piper had never taken with a man she barely knew. "Lead the way."

No sooner had she said it than he clasped her hand and guided her toward another closed door where he paused to kiss her again. When his palms roved along her rib cage before they came to rest on her bottom, she found it very difficult to breathe.

He suddenly broke all contact and took a step back. "There is something I need to say before we go any further."

Piper managed to break through the sensual fog and back into reality. "You're married."

"Of course not."

That left only one scenario as far as she could see. "If you're worried that I'm making some alcohol-induced decision, you're wrong. Yes, I've had a couple of drinks, but I'm not drunk. And yes, this strangers-in-the-night scenario is a first for me. In fact, I've only had one lover, and even calling him that is a stretch."

He seemed totally confused by that concept. "How is that possible for such an appealing woman?"

"Believe me, it is possible because I'm very particular."

"I am flattered, yet I still question whether you are giving this enough thought."

She didn't want to think, only do. "Look, in a perfect world, I'd suggest we spend a few days getting to know each other before we take this step. But unfortunately I was informed only a few hours ago that I'm traveling to some obscure Middle Eastern country to schmooze with sheikhs for the sake of trying to win a water conservation contract."

His expression went stone-cold serious. "Are you referring to the Mehdis?"

"Yes, and I realize they're your friends, but—"

"We need to talk."

That meant only one thing—party's over. "All right," she muttered, unable to mask the disappointment in her voice.

A.J. led her to the white sofa set out in the middle of the room. After they settled on the cushions side by side, he took both her hands into his. "You are one of the most beautiful, intelligent and intriguing women I have met in a very long time. Quite simply, you're special. For that reason, I do not want to take advantage of you."

Take advantage of me, dammit, she wanted to say, but opted for a more subtle debate. "I'm not special at all. However, I'm sure you normally require an experienced partner, and if it's that's your concern, I'm much more adventurous than I seem. I think my being in your hotel room is a sure sign of that."

He released her hands and leaned back. "As much as I would like to find out, I'd prefer not to complicate matters, which leads me to what I need to tell you. I pilot the Mehdis' plane."

Her eyes widened from sheer shock. "Why didn't you tell me this in the beginning?"

"It didn't matter until you said you'd be working with them. If the king learned I was bedding a prospective client, he would, simply put, go ballistic."

Figured. "Leave it to some well-heeled royal to spoil my good time. That's why I have no use for that kind of man."

His gaze wandered away. "He would be justified in his condemnation. I have a responsibility to the Mehdis and a need to be taken seriously by them."

"At all costs?"

"I'm afraid that is the case at this point in time."

In other words, thanks but no thanks, or at least that was what Piper heard. Feeling somewhat humiliated, she came to her feet. "It's been a pleasure to meet you, A.J. Thank you for a very lovely and eye-opening evening."

Before she had a meltdown, Piper headed away, only to be stopped by A.J. bracing her shoulders from behind before she could open the door.

He turned her to face him, his expression extremely solemn. "Piper, there are two things you must know about me. First, I have been taught that a man is only as good as his honor, and I am trying to honor you, even if I would like to take that black dress off you and carry you to my bed. Despite my concerns about my job, you also deserve the utmost respect and regard. And once you have time to consider my decision, you will thank me for saving you from a possible mistake."

For some reason that made Piper a little miffed. "Do you honestly believe I don't know my own mind?"

"I believe you're too trusting."

Now she was just plain mad. "I'm an adult, A.J., not some naive adolescent. And in case you're worried, I'm not a prude, I'm picky. Last, the only mistake I made tonight was thinking you could be the man who would be worth the wait. Obviously I was wrong."

He softly touched her face. "You are not wrong. When it comes to us—" he twined their fingers together, sending a message that wasn't lost on Piper "—making love, I assure you that would definitely be worth the wait. And that is what I'm proposing, waiting until we have the opportunity to know each other while you are in Bajul."

Piper's anger almost disappeared. Almost. "That would depend on whether you're everything you seem to be, because I believe honesty *and* honor go hand in hand. Now, what was the second thing you wanted me to know?"

A strange look passed over his face. "I still believe in chivalry. Will you allow me to walk you to your room?"

She shook her head. "No, thanks. I'm a big girl and I can find my way."

"As you wish." After he escorted her into the corridor, A.J. executed a slight bow. "If I don't see you tomorrow on the plane, Ms. McAdams, then I will make it a point to seek you out in Bajul."

She boarded the extremely large and lavish private plane less than five minutes before their scheduled departure, due to the rush-hour traffic and an apathetic cabdriver. When the five-man survey crew settled into the vacant beige leather seats at the front of the plane, she walked the aisle past what she assumed to be staff and press members. Despite the size of the plane, it appeared the back half had been cordoned off to passengers. Most likely it held a series of conference rooms and perhaps even living quarters. She might ask A.J. to give her the grand tour, provided she actually encountered him before they landed.

She paused in the aisle to address a middle-aged, professor-like man with sparse graying hair, wire-rimmed glasses and kind brown eyes. Hopefully he spoke English, and that the last remaining spot was available. "Is this seat taken?"

"It is reserved for Miss McAdams," he replied. "Is that you?"

Fortunately a language barrier wouldn't exist during the lengthy flight. "Yes, that's me."

"Then the seat is yours."

After sliding in next to the man and settling her red tote at her feet, she shifted toward him and stuck out her hand. "Hello, I'm Piper McAdams. I'm traveling to Bajul with the GLM engineers."

He gave her hand a soft shake. "Mr. Deeb."

Not a lot to go on there. Time for a fishing expedition. "Are you a friend of the sheikh's?"

"I am serving as his attaché on this trip."

"I'm sure that's a very interesting duty."

He pushed his glasses up on the bridge of his nose. "Managing Prince Adan's schedule can be challenging at times, evidenced by his absence at the moment."

A good thing, since she might have missed the flight if the guy had been punctual. "He has a habit of being late, does he?"

"He occasionally suffers from tardiness, among other things."

Piper wanted him to define "other things" but then she noticed a commotion toward the front of the plane. Assuming the mysterious monarch had finally arrived, she came to her feet along with the rest of the passengers and leaned slightly into the aisle to catch a glimpse. She spotted only A.J. dressed in a crisp, white shirt covered by a navy blue suit emblazoned with gold military-like insignias. Not a sheikh in sight.

She regarded Mr. Deeb again and lowered her voice. "He must be some kind of pilot to earn that reception."

He cleared his throat and glanced away. "Yes, he is quite the aviator."

After everyone settled into their seats, Piper followed suit, well aware that her pulse had unwittingly picked up speed as she noticed A.J. stopping in the aisle to speak to one man. A man who oddly addressed the pilot as Prince Adan.

Reality soon dawned, along with the sense that she might have been completely betrayed by blind faith. She turned a frown on Mr. Deeb. "He's not the plane's pilot, is he?"

Again the man refused to look at her directly. "Yes, he is the pilot, as well as commander in chief of Bajul's armed forces."

"And a Mehdi?"

Deeb gave her a contrite look. "The third Mehdi son in line to inherit the throne."

And a major liar, Piper realized as she watched the sheikh disappear into the cockpit. She thanked her lucky stars she hadn't made the mistake of climbing into bed with him. Then again, he'd been the one to put an end to that with his fake concerns over being only a royal employee, not a royal prince. And all that talk of honor. Honorable men didn't deceive unsuspecting women about their identities.

Fuming over the duplicity, Piper pulled a fashion magazine from her bag and flipped through the pages with a vengeance during takeoff. She didn't have to deal with the situation now, or ever for that matter. She didn't have to spend even one minute with A.J. or Adan or whatever his name was. He would be nothing more to her than a cute meet that had gone nowhere, a precautionary tale in the book of her life, a man she would endeavor to immediately forget....

"May I have a moment with you in the aft lounge, Ms. McAdams?"

She glanced up and immediately took in A.J.'s damnable dimples and his sexy mouth before visually traveling to his remarkable dark eyes. "Is the plane flying itself, *Prince* Mehdi?"

He tried on a contrite look. "I have turned the controls over to the copilot for the time being so we can converse."

And if she spent one second alone with him, she

might find herself caught up in his lair once more. "I do believe the seat belt sign is still on, and that means it's not safe to move about the cabin."

Of course said sign picked that moment to ding and dim, robbing her of any excuse to avoid this confrontation. Nevertheless, he happened to be resident royalty, not to mention he could hold the power to grant—or reject—her grandfather's bid. For that reason, she shoved the magazine back into the carry-on and slid out of the seat, putting her in very close proximity to the fibbing prince. "After you," she said in a tone that was borderline irritable, to say the least.

As the princely pilot started toward the rear of the plane, Piper followed behind him with her eyes lowered in an attempt to avoid the two female attendants' curious stares. He paused to open a sliding frosted-glass door and gestured her forward into a narrow corridor before he showed her into a lounge containing dark brown leather furniture.

"Make yourself comfortable," A.J. said as he closed the sliding door behind her.

Comfortable? Ha! Piper chose the lone chair to avoid inadvertent physical contact, while the sneaky sheikh settled on the opposing sofa.

He draped his arm casually over the back cushions and smiled. "Have you enjoyed your flight so far?"

In an effort to demonstrate some decorum, she bit back the harsh words clamoring to come out of her mouth. "Since it's been less than fifteen minutes into the flight, I prefer to reserve judgment until landing."

He gave her a lingering once-over. "You look very beautiful today, Piper."

She tugged the hem of her black coatdress down to

the top of her knees. Unfortunately she couldn't convert the open collar to a turtleneck. "Thank you, but if you believe compliments will put you in the clear after you lied to me, think again."

"I am being completely sincere in my admiration."

"Forgive me if I question your sincerity. And by the way, what am I supposed to call you?"

"What would you like to call me?"

He'd walked right into that one. "Jackass?"

He had the audacity to grin. "I believe I have been called that before."

She had the utterly stupid urge to kiss that grin off his face. "I don't doubt that a bit. And where did you come up with A.J.?"

"My given name is Adan Jamal. My classmates called me A.J., but as an adult I do prefer Adan."

"I would have preferred you explain all of this to me last night."

His expression turned serious. "When I discovered you were involved with the water project, I was completely thrown off-kilter."

Not a valid excuse, in her opinion. "And after learning that, did you seriously believe you could hide your identity from me indefinitely?"

He sighed. "No. I had hoped to speak with you before takeoff. Unfortunately, traffic detained our driver on the way to the airport and I had to adhere to the original flight plan."

She couldn't reject that defense when she'd experienced the same delays. Still… "You still should have told me before I left your room, at the very least."

He leaned forward, draped his elbows on his parted knees and studied the carpeted floor. "Do you know what it's like to be judged by your station in life even though it has nothing to do with who you really are?"

Actually, she did—the rich girl born to a spoiled, partying socialite and an unknown father. "I can relate to that in some ways."

He finally raised his gaze to hers. "Last night, I wanted you to see me as an average man, not a monarch."

There was absolutely nothing average about him. "I don't base my opinions on a person's social status."

He straightened and streaked a palm over his shadowed jaw. "I believe I recall you mentioning you have an aversion to wealthy men, and specifically, the Mehdis. Is that not so?"

Darned if he wasn't right. "Okay, yes, I might have said that. My apologies for making generalizations."

"And I apologize for deceiving you. I promise it will not happen again, as soon as I tell you something else I omitted last evening."

Just when she thought she might be able to trust him. "I'm listening."

"I've been celibate since my eldest brother's wedding."

"When was that?" she asked around her surprise.

"Eight months ago and approximately two months following the dissolution of my relationship."

Piper couldn't imagine such a vital, viral man could go that long without sex. "Your breakup must have been really devastating."

"Not exactly," he said. "My brothers have always seen me as being less than serious when it comes to my role in the family. I decided to prove to them that my entire life does not revolve around seeking the next conquest."

She so wanted to believe him, yet wasn't certain she could. "I admire your resolve, but I'm still having a hard time with the trust issue where you're concerned."

Adan came to his feet, crossed the small space between them, clasped her hands and pulled her off the chair. "I must see to my responsibility now as captain of this ship. But before I go, I have a request."

Who knew what that might entail? "Go ahead."

"If you will allow me to serve as your personal host in Bajul, I will prove to you that I am not only a man of my word, but I am an honorable man."

That remained to be seen. But right then, when Adan Mehdi looked at her as if she deserved his utmost attention, she couldn't manufacture one reason to refuse his hospitality. And if she didn't keep a cool head, she worried he could convince her of anything.

"Ms. Thorpe is here to see you, Emir."

Great. He'd barely walked into the palace with Piper at his side only to be greeted by an unwelcome visit from his past in the form of a persistent, self-absorbed ex-paramour.

The entire travel party scattered like rats on a sinking ship, including the turncoat Deeb. Only the messenger of doom remained, an extremely perplexed look splashed across his bearded face. "Did you know she was coming, Abdul?"

The man revealed his discomfort by wringing his hands. "No, Emir. I attempted to ask her to return tomorrow, yet she would not hear of it. She is currently in the study with…uh…those who accompanied her. It would be in your best interest to speak with her."

Leave it to Talia to bring an entourage. And if she created a scene, he would never earn Piper's trust. Therefore he had to find a way to keep the two women separated.

With that in mind, Adan turned to Piper and gestured toward the towering staircase leading to the upper floors. "This shouldn't take too long, Ms. McAdams. In the meantime, Abdul will show you to your quarters and I will meet you shortly in the third-floor sitting room. Abdul, put her things in the suite across from mine."

After Abdul picked up her luggage, she didn't make a move other than to give Adan a decidedly suspicious stare. "I have a room reserved at the inn in the village, so it's best I keep those arrangements, Your Highness," she said, prompting the houseman to set the bags back down.

He had to encourage her to stay at the palace, and he had limited time to do so. After signaling Abdul to gather the bags again, he regarded Piper. "The inn is small and will not allow you to have what you need in terms of your business. They currently do not have internet access or an office center. We have all that here."

Abdul bent slightly as if prepared to return the luggage to the floor while Adan tamped down his impatience over Piper's delay in responding. "I suppose you have a point," she finally said. "As long as it's not an inconvenience for your staff."

He would be inconvenienced if he didn't have her nearby, and in deep trouble if the old girlfriend suddenly made an appearance. "I assure you, the staff is accustomed to guests. So if you will follow Abdul—"

"It's about time you finally showed up, you inconsiderate arse."

Adan froze like an iceberg at the sound of the familiar voice. Trouble had definitely arrived.

He could pretend he hadn't heard her, or he could face the unavoidable confrontation like a man. Taking the second—and least palatable—option, he turned to discover Talia Thorpe standing at the entry to the hallway wearing a chic white dress, hands propped on her narrow hips and her green eyes alight with fury.

A compliment should help to diffuse the possible verbal bloodbath. Or so he hoped. "You're looking well, Talia."

She rolled her eyes. "Why haven't you returned my emails or calls? I've sent you at least a hundred messages over the past month alone."

He ventured a fast glance at Piper, who appeared to be somewhat taken aback, and rightfully so. "Might I remind you, Talia, we broke off our relationship a year ago."

Talia tossed a lock of her long platinum hair back over one shoulder. "*You* broke it off, and it's been ten months. If you hadn't ignored me, I wouldn't have been forced to disrupt my schedule and make this beastly trip."

When he'd told her they were done after their on-and-off six-year relationship, he'd meant it. "Perhaps we should continue this conversation somewhere more private."

She flipped a manicured hand in Piper's direction. "Are you worried your new chicky will be exposed to all the dirty details?"

As a matter of fact… "For your information, Ms. McAdams is here on business."

"Well, so am I," Talia said. "Serious business."

He wouldn't be at all surprised if she tried to sue him over the breakup. "I find that somewhat difficult to believe, Talia, yet I am curious. What business of yours would concern me?"

She turned around and clapped her hands. "Bridget, you may come in now and bring it with you."

Talia went through personal assistants as frequently as she went through money, so Adan wasn't surprised when he didn't recognize the name. He was mildly concerned over the "it" comment. But he was nothing less than astounded when the meek-looking plump brunette strolled into the room…gripping a baby carrier. Myriad concerns began rushing through his mind. Unthinkable possibilities. Unimaginable scenarios.

Yet when Talia took the carrier and turned it around, and he saw the sleeping baby with the tiny round face and the black cap of hair, he would swear his heart skipped several beats, and he began to sweat.

"Adan, meet Samuel, your new son."

Three

Piper wouldn't be a bit surprised if Adan Mehdi keeled over from shock. Instead, he assumed a rigid posture and a stern expression, hands fisted at his sides. "Talia, if you believe I will simply take you at your word about this, you are completely daft."

The woman swept her manicured hand toward the infant. "Just look at him, Adan. You can't deny he's yours. Dark hair and golden skin. He even has your dimples. Despite all that, I do have proof in the form of a DNA test."

"How did you get my bloody DNA?" he asked.

Talia crossed her arms beneath her breasts and lifted her chin. "It's all over my Paris flat, Adan. And you happened to leave your toothbrush the night you tossed me to the gutter."

The sheikh's defenses seemed to disappear right before Piper's eyes. "We were always careful to prevent pregnancy."

Talia tapped her chin. "I do recall that one night last year in Milan—"

"That was one blasted night, Talia," he replied, his tone fraught with anger.

"Once was quite enough." The woman handed the carrier off to a bewildered Bridget. "Anyway, I have a photo shoot in a remote location in Tasmania, which will give you an opportunity to get to know your kid. We'll discuss the custody particulars when I get back next month."

Adan narrowed his eyes in a menacing glare. "We will discuss this immediately."

Talia checked her watch. "My flight leaves in less than an hour."

"You will not take one step out this door until we talk," Adan demanded. "Into the study. Now."

After the sheikh and his former girlfriend exited, Piper looked around to find Abdul had disappeared, leaving her in a quandary over what to do next. She occupied her time by surveying the beige stone walls, the ornate gold statues and the unending staircase leading to the top of the massive structure. A baby's cry would definitely echo loudly throughout the building.

With that in mind, Piper sought out Bridget, who'd taken a seat on the gold brocade cushioned bench set against the wall, the carrier at her feet. She smiled at the woman, who managed a slight, albeit shaky return of the gesture. But when the baby began to fuss, the presumed au pair looked completely alarmed.

Not good. Piper launched into action, crossed to the carrier, unfolded the yellow blanket, picked up the crying infant and held him against her shoulder. After he quieted, she regarded the wide-eyed Bridget. "You aren't a nanny, are you?"

"No, I am not," she finally responded, her tone hinting at a slight British accent and a lot of disdain. "I'm Talia's personal assistant. The last nanny quit yesterday when she learned she'd have to make the trip here. Traveling with Talia isn't pleasant under normal circumstances, let alone with a child in tow."

Piper claimed the vacant spot on the bench, laid the swaddled baby in the crook of her arm and studied his cherub face. "You're beautiful, little man, although you don't look like a Samuel. Sam fits you better."

"Don't let Talia hear you call him that," Bridget warned. "She fired the first nanny over that very thing."

That didn't exactly surprise Piper after what she'd witnessed upon meeting the model. "Then she's very protective of him, huh?"

Bridget frowned. "Not really. She hasn't held him more than a handful of times since his birth."

Piper couldn't contain her contempt, a product of her own experience. "Good mothers hold and care for their babies. They certainly don't foist their children off on someone else."

Bridget reached over and touched the infant's arm. "You're right, but unfortunately Talia isn't maternal. She's consumed by her modeling career and staying in shape. All I've heard since his birth is how hard she's had to work to regain her figure. I truly believe that's why she waited four weeks to bring the baby here."

Vanity, thy name is Talia. She was beginning to like her less and less. "At least now he'll have the opportunity to bond with his father."

"I am not prepared to raise a child, Talia."

So much for bonding, Piper thought at the sound of the sheikh's irritated tone.

The self-centered supermodel breezed into the room with one impatient prince following close on her heels. "At least you didn't have to suffer through thirteen hours of horrible labor last month. And just imagine pushing a soccer ball out your todger. Besides, you have a whole staff to assist you while I had to hire several useless nannies over the past month. Good help is hard to find."

"Perhaps that's because you have no idea how to treat the help," Adan muttered as he strode into the vestibule.

Talia turned and set an oversize light blue bag next to the carrier, affording Piper only a cursory glance. "Bridget gave him a bottle three hours ago, so no doubt he'll be hungry again very soon. There's enough nappies, bottles and cans of formula in here to get you by until tomorrow, plus a few outfits. After that, you're on your own. Let's go, Bridget."

Without giving the baby even a passing glance, much less a kiss goodbye, Talia headed for the door with poor Bridget cowering behind her. Piper practically bit a hole in her tongue against the urge to deliver a seething diatribe aimed at the woman's disregard for her child. Instead, she shifted Sam back to her shoulder and remained silent as Adan followed the two women to the entry and accompanied them out the door.

When the baby began to whimper again, Piper assumed he was probably in need of another bottle. Fortunately, feeding an infant wasn't an issue, even if it had been a while since her teenage babysitting days— the one job her grandparents had allowed her to accept, but only in a limited capacity, and exclusively for those parents who'd run in their social circle.

Piper laid Sam vertically in her lap, rummaged through the bag, withdrew a bottle and uncapped it. He took the nipple without hesitation and suckled with great enthusiasm, complete with soft, yummy noises that brought about her smile. After he drained the formula in record time, she set the empty bottle beside her, returned him to her shoulder and rubbed his back to successfully burp him. Then she cradled him in the crook of her arm and stroked his cotton-soft cheek. For a time he stared at her with an unfocused gaze before planting his right thumb in his rosebud mouth.

As his eyes drifted closed, Piper experienced sheer empathy for this precious little boy. She couldn't fathom how anyone would reject such a gift. Couldn't imagine how any mother worth her salt would simply drop off her child with a man who hadn't even known he had a son. Then again, why should she be surprised? Her very own mother had abandoned her and Sunny with their grandparents shortly after their birth. As far as she was concerned, women like Talia Thorpe and Millicent McAdams should not be allowed to procreate.

Despite her poor maternal example, Piper had always dreamed of having children of her own. So far she hadn't found a suitable candidate to father her future offspring, and she certainly wasn't going to settle for anything less than a loving relationship with a man who had the same wants and desires. A gentle, caring man. Grounded. Settled…

"I am officially moving to Antarctica."

After the declaration, Adan strode past Piper and disappeared into the nearby corridor adjacent to the

towering staircase. Again. Granted, she enjoyed holding baby Sam, but she hadn't signed on to be the royal
nursemaid. And apparently the sheikh hadn't signed up
for fatherhood, either.

A few moments passed before Adan returned with a
petite, attractive older woman wearing an impeccable
navy tailored blazer and skirt, her salt-and-pepper hair
styled in a neat bob. Yet when she caught sight of Piper
and the baby, her pleasant demeanor melted into obvious confusion. "May I help you, miss?"

"This is Piper McAdams," Adan said. "She has accompanied the survey crew, and while she's here, she
will be my guest. Piper, this is Elena Battelli, my former governess who now governs the entire household."

Piper came to her feet and smiled. "It's very nice to
meet you."

"And I, you." Elena leaned over and studied the baby.
"What a lovely child you have. Boy or girl?"

"He's Talia's child," Adan interjected before Piper
had a chance to respond.

Elena's initial shock melted into an acid look. "Is
that dreadful woman here?"

"She has departed for now," Adan said. "And she left
this infant in my charge before she left the premises."

Now the governess appeared completely appalled.
"She expects you to care for her child?"

The sheikh looked somewhat contrite before he re-
gained his commanding demeanor. "He is mine, Elena."

Piper really wanted to take the baby and bail before the verbal fireworks began. "If you two would like
some privacy—"

"You have no reason to leave," Adan said. "You have
already witnessed the worst of the situation."

Elena's features turned as stern as a practiced head-mistress. "How long have you known about this child, *cara*? And how can you be certain that woman is being truthful?"

Adan streaked a palm over his neck. "I didn't know until today, and she provided the test results that prove I am his father. Now, before you begin the lecture, I have a few things I need you to do."

The woman straightened her shoulders and stared at him. "This is your bed, Adan Mehdi, and you will lie in it. So if you expect me to raise your son—"

"I do not expect that at all," Adan replied. "In fact, I intend to take complete control over his care until his mother returns."

Provided the missing model did come back, Piper's major concern. But at the moment, she had a more pressing issue that needed to be addressed. "Do you think you might like to hold your son first, Your Highness?"

Uncertainty called out from Adan's brown eyes as he slowly approached her. "I suppose that would be the most logical next step."

Piper turned the baby around and placed him in his father's arms. "I promise he's not going to break," she added when she noted his slight look of concern.

While the sheikh held his son for the first time, the former governess stood next to him, one hand resting on Adan's shoulder. "He looks exactly like you did at his age, *cara*," she said in a reverent tone. "Such a *bella* baby. Does he have a name?"

"Sam," Piper chimed in without thought. "Actually, Samuel, but I think he looks more like a Sam. Or maybe Sammy." When she noticed Adan's disapprov-

ing glance, she amended that decision. "Sammy definitely doesn't work. Of course, what you call him is
solely up to you."

"He will eventually be renamed in accordance with
tradition," Adan said, sounding very authoritative and
princely. "Right now I must see to his comfort, including finding him a suitable crib."

"The nursery is still in order," Elena said. "And since
your brother and Madison are currently residing at their
home in the States, you may use it. We still have several bottles in the pantry, and a few items in the cupboard in the nursery, but I'm afraid we have no diapers
or formula since the twins have moved past that stage.
But the cribs are still there and fully equipped with
blankets and such."

Adan appeared somewhat perplexed. "The nursery
is down the hall from my quarters. I will not be able to
hear him if he needs me during the night."

The governess took the baby without permission,
and without protest, from the fledgling father, a sure
sign of her close bond with the youngest Mehdi son.
"There is something known as a baby monitor, *cara*.
You will be able to see and hear him at any time when
you are in your suite."

"Have the monitor set up in my room," he said. "I
will see to the supplies tomorrow. You mentioned Zain
is in Los Angeles, but you have not said anything about
Rafiq."

Rafiq Mehdi, the reigning king of Bajul, and reportedly a hard case, according to her grandfather. Piper
would buy tickets to see his reaction to the current scandal. Then again, maybe not. She'd had enough drama
for one day.

Elena continued to stare at the baby with the reverence of a grandmother. "Rafiq has been with his wife at the resort for the past week. They will not be returning for two more days."

Adan shrugged out of his jacket and hung it on an ornately carved coat tree in the vestibule before returning to them. "Make certain Rafiq knows nothing about this until I have the opportunity to speak with him."

When she recognized a serious problem with that request, Piper decided to add her two cents. "Can you trust the household staff to keep this quiet?"

"The staff knows to exercise complete confidentially," Elena said.

"Or suffer the consequences," Adan added gruffly before turning to the governess. "Please have Abdul deliver the monitor and our bags to our rooms, and watch him while I show Ms. McAdams to her quarters."

Elena kissed the baby's forehead. "I have no reason to watch Abdul, *cara*. I trust he'll do as he's told."

After Adan muttered something in Arabic that didn't sound exactly pleasant, Piper stifled a laugh and considered an offer. "I have no problem watching the baby while you settle in, Your Highness."

"That will not be necessary, Ms. McAdams," Elena said as she handed the baby back to Adan. "If you are bent on being a good father to your son, then you should begin immediately."

Adan looked slightly panicked. "But—"

"No buts, Adan Mehdi." The governess snatched the empty bottle from the bench before addressing Piper again. "Ms. McAdams, it was certainly a pleasure to meet you, even under such unusual circumstances. I shall go instruct Abdul while the royal pilot becomes accustomed to paternity. Please let me know if you need any assistance with the boy."

Piper returned her smile. "Luckily I babysat quite a few times in my youth, so we'll be fine."

"Actually, I was referring to my former charge, the prince."

The two women shared a laugh before Elena walked away, leaving Piper alone with Adan and his son.

"She treats me as if I still wear knickers," he said, frustration evident in his tone.

Piper moved to his side and peeked at the still sleeping infant. "Evidently the two of you are very close, and I honestly believe she has your best interests at heart."

He released a rough sigh. "I suppose she does, at that. Now, if you're ready, I shall escort you to your room before I settle the baby into the nursery."

Piper almost insisted on returning to the inn, yet when she saw a trace of doubt in Adan's eyes, the touch of awkwardness as he held his child, the sympathy bug bit her. "Why don't we put him in the carrier while we climb the stairs?"

"No need," he said. "If you'll be so kind as to gather his things, I'll show you to the private elevator."

Piper couldn't help but smile over Adan's decision not to relinquish his son. Maybe she'd underestimated his ability to move into his new role after all.

He had untold riches at his disposal. He could fly jets at warp speed, navigate treacherous mountain slopes on skis and answer a woman's most secret fantasies with little effort. Yet he had no idea what to do with an infant.

As he studied the child in his arms, Adan's own paternal experience fueled his drive to succeed in this endeavor. He'd often wondered if the man who'd claimed him—and in many ways discarded him—had actually been his biological father. That question had always haunted him and always would. He vowed to give his son everything he would ever need, including his undivided attention.

His son. He'd never believed he would be in this position at this point in his life. Yet he was, and he had no one else to blame for his carelessness. No one to truly count on but himself.

"Is this where we get off, Your Highness?"

Until Piper had spoken, he hadn't noticed the car had come to a stop. "It is." After he moved through the open doors, he faced her in the corridor. "I respectfully request you call me Adan when we're in private."

She shifted the tote's strap to her shoulder. "All right, as long as you don't mind me referring to your son as Sam."

Clearly the woman was a born negotiator. "If that pleases you, I agree. I, however, will call him Samuel until he is renamed."

She sent him a satisfied smile. "It greatly pleases me, Adan."

Under different circumstances, he would definitely like to please her in other, more intimate ways. Then his son began to whimper, reminding him those carefree days were all but over. "Do you think he is hungry again?"

"I think he's probably wet," she said. "I also think we should stop by the nursery first and check it out."

A good plan. At least she could assist him when he took his first venture into diaper changing.

Piper followed behind him as he traveled the lengthy

hallway past several unoccupied guest suites. He stopped immediately right of the staircase landing and opened the door to the nursery that he had once occupied with his two brothers almost thirty years ago. The room had been left much the same, with two cribs and a small single bed set against the sand-colored walls, a large blue trunk holding the toys from his early childhood positioned in the corner. The miniature round table and chairs were still centered in the room, the place where Elena had taught the boys lessons as well as her native language, Italian. Where she had read to them nightly before bedtime in lieu of the mother Adan had never known. But that had lasted only until he'd turned six years old, when he'd been unceremoniously shipped off to boarding school.

The baby's cries began to escalate, thrusting the bittersweet memories away. He stepped aside to allow Piper entry, plagued by a sudden sense of absolute helplessness when he couldn't think of a blasted thing to do to calm his son. He hated failure in any form, and he'd worked hard to succeed in nearly everything he'd endeavored. Yet somehow this miniature human had left him virtually defenseless.

Piper crossed the room to the dressing table and set the tote and carrier at her feet. "Bring him over here."

"Gladly."

After he laid the infant on the white cushioned surface, Samuel continued to wail at a decibel that could possibly summon the palace guards. Piper seemed willing to speed up the process by sliding the yellow-footed pajama bottoms down the infant's legs. She then leaned down to retrieve a diaper that she set on the end of the table. "You can take it from here."

While the child continued to cry, Adan surveyed the plastic contraption and tried to recall a time when he'd watched his sister-in-law change one of the twins. Sadly, he could not. "I am not well versed in proper diaper-changing procedure."

Piper sighed. "First, you need to remove the wet diaper by releasing the tapes. But I need to warn you about something first."

He suspected it wouldn't be the last child-rearing caution he would hear. "Take care not to flip him on his head?"

She frowned. "Well, obviously that, and make sure you're ready to hold the diaper back in place if he's not done. Otherwise, you could find yourself being anointed in the face."

He certainly had never considered that. "How do you know these things?"

She withdrew a white container from the bag and opened it to reveal some sort of paper wipes. "I learned the hard way. I used to babysit for a family with three boys, and two of them were in diapers."

This woman—who had been a stranger to him twenty-four hours ago—could very well be his savior. After he lowered the diaper and didn't have to dodge, he readied for the next step. "Now what?"

"Gently grasp his ankles with one hand, lift his bottom, then slide the diaper from beneath him with your free hand."

Adan had earned a degree in aeronautics, yet this task seemed astronomical. Fortunately the boy found his thumb to pacify himself while his fumbling father figured out the process. And thankfully his hand easily circled both the infant's ankles, and raising his legs was akin to lifting a feather. Once he had the diaper removed and the baby lowered, he turned back to Piper. "Piece of cake."

She took the plastic garment from him and discarded it in the nearby bin. "True, but he's still little. Just realize there will soon come a time when he'll be much more mobile, and a lot less cooperative."

The image of his child vaulting from the dressing table assaulted him. "Will I need to strap him down?"

Piper laughed. "You'll have enough experience by then to handle him. And you'll probably want to change him in a place that's a little lower to the ground."

He shook his head. "I had no idea that caring for someone so small would require so much knowledge. I am ill equipped for the task."

"You're more than equipped, Adan." She handed him a damp paper cloth, set the container aside, then grabbed the clean diaper and unfolded it. "But right now your son requires that you finish this task. After you clean him up a bit, repeat the first step, only this time slide the diaper underneath him."

Piper displayed great patience as he followed her instructions to the letter. Once he had the infant rediapered and redressed, he noticed that his son had fallen asleep.

"Grab the bag and we'll put this little guy to bed," Piper said as she lifted the baby, crossed the room and placed him on his back in one of the two cribs.

Tote in hand, Adan came to her side. As he watched his child sleep, he experienced a strong sense of pride. "I must say he's quite something."

"Yes he is," she replied in a hushed tone. "Now let's

go so he can have a decent nap before it's feeding time again."

After one last look at his son, Adan guided Piper into the corridor, leaving the nursery room door ajar. "Do you think it's all right to leave him all alone in an unfamiliar place?"

She patted his arm and smiled. "He's going to be fine for the next hour or so. And I'm sure Elena will have the monitor in place very soon so you can track his every move. But you will need to send out for supplies tomorrow."

"I prefer to take care of the supplies myself," he said on a whim. "However, I could use some counsel on what to purchase, if you would be so kind as to accompany me into the village. I can also show you the sights while we're there."

"Aren't you afraid someone might recognize you?"

He was more afraid she would reject his plan to spend more time with her. "I have ways to disguise myself to avoid recognition. We would appear to be tourists exploring the town."

She hid a yawn behind her hands. "I could probably do that. But at the moment, I could use a nap. Jet lag has taken hold of me."

What an inconsiderate buffoon he'd become. "Of course. If you'll follow me, I will show you to your quarters."

Adan guided Piper toward the suite opposite his, situated two rooms down from the nursery. Once there, he opened the door and she breezed past him, coming to a stop at the end of the queen-size bed. He stepped inside and watched as she surveyed the room before facing the open windows that revealed the mountains in the distance.

"This is a beautiful view," she said without turning around.

"Yes, it is." And he wasn't referring to the panoramic scenery. She was beautiful. Incredibly beautiful, from the top of her hair that ruffled in the warm breeze, to her man-slaying high heels, and all points in between. What he wouldn't give to divest her of that black dress, lay her down on the purple silk bedspread and have his wicked way with her....

"That peak is really prominent."

She had no idea, and he was thankful she hadn't turned around to find out. After regaining some composure, he crossed the room and moved behind her. "The largest mountain is called Mabrúuk. Legend has it that it blesses Bajul with fertility."

She turned, putting them in close proximity. "Fertile as in crops?"

"Actually, livestock and village offspring. We've come to know it as the baby-making mountain."

She smiled. "Did its powers reach all the way to Milan?"

"Perhaps so."

Her smile disappeared, replaced by self-consciousness. "I'm sorry. I shouldn't have brought that up. Obviously you were shocked over learning you had a son."

An understatement of the first order. "Yes, but I am in part responsible. If I had answered Talia's messages, I would have known much sooner. But I frankly did not have the desire to speak with her after we broke off the relationship. Six years of Talia's antics had been quite enough."

"And that brings me to a question," she said, followed by, "if you don't mind me asking."

After all his talk of honor, she deserved to grill him as much as she would like. "Ask away."

"Why were you with Talia all that time if you found her intolerable?"

A very good question. "In all honesty, my attraction to her was purely physical. But in defense of Talia, she has not had an easy life. She practically raised herself in the back alleys of London after her mother died and her father drowned his sorrows in the local pubs. Beneath that tough and somewhat haughty exterior resides a lost little girl who fears poverty and a loss of pride."

Piper released a caustic laugh. "Sorry, but that doesn't excuse her for bringing a baby into the world and basically ignoring him after the fact."

He recalled the recent conversation he'd had with Talia in the study. "She told me she had considered giving Samuel up for adoption, but she also felt I had a right to decide if I wanted to be a part of his life."

"And she thought springing him on you was the way to handle that?"

"Talia is nothing if not spontaneous. And as I've said, I refused to answer any correspondence."

She sighed. "Look, I know it's really none of my business, but I suspect she could be using Sam as a pawn to get you back into her life."

"Or perhaps for monetary gain," he said, regretfully voicing his own suspicions.

Piper reacted with a scowl. "She wants you to buy your own son from her?"

"She did not exactly say that, but it is a possibility. And if that proves to be true, I would willingly give her any amount of money for the opportunity to raise my child without her interference."

Her features brightened. "I admire your conviction, Adan. Sam is lucky to have you as his dad."

She could have offered him an accommodation for bravery in battle and it would not have meant as much. "And I appreciate your faith in me, Piper. Yet I am well aware of the challenges ahead of me."

She favored him with a grin that traveled to her diamond-blue eyes. "Just wait until you have to give him a bath this evening."

That sent several horrific images shooting through his muddled mind. "Bloody hell, what if I drop him?"

She patted his cheek. "You won't if you're careful. And I'll be there to show you how it's done."

He caught her hand and brought it against his chest. "You have been a godsend, Piper McAdams. And you now hold the distinction of being the most attractive tutor I have ever encountered."

"Then we're even," she said, her voice soft and overtly sensuous.

He tugged her closer. "In what way?"

She wrested out of his grasp and draped her arms around his neck. "You happen to be the best kisser I've ever encountered to this point."

He wanted to kiss her now. Needed to kiss her now. And he did—without any compunction whatsoever, regardless of his responsibility to his sleeping son. With a bed very close at hand and her heady response to the thrust of his tongue, all reasoning flew out the open windows.

"Excuse me, Emir."

Abdul's voice was as effective as having ice water

poured down one's pants, thrusting Adan away from Piper. He tried to clear the uncomfortable hitch from his throat before facing the servant. "Yes, Abdul?"

"I have Ms. McAdams's luggage."

"Then bring it in."

The man set the bags at the end of the bed, then executed a slight bow before hurrying away and closing the door behind him, something Adan should have done to avoid the predicament.

He sent Piper an apologetic look. "I am very sorry I did not see to our privacy."

She touched her fingertips to her lips. "We really shouldn't be doing this."

The declaration sent his good spirits into a nosedive. "Why not?"

"Because I can't help but wonder exactly how much you really knew about Talia's pregnancy."

This time when she called his honor into question, he responded with fury. "I did not even remotely suspect she might be pregnant. Otherwise this issue would have been resolved in the beginning. And it pains me to know you hold me in such low esteem that you think I would abandon my own child."

"I'm sorry," she said quietly. "That was an unfair assumption since you seem so willing to care for your son."

His anger diminished when he noted the sincerity in her voice. "You do have every right to doubt me, Piper, in light of my initial fabrications. But I swear to you again that I will do everything in my power to prove my honor."

She answered with a slight smile. "After meeting that

man-eater, Talia, I now understand why you might be driven straight into celibacy."

That vow was the last thing on his mind after he'd kissed Piper. "As I've said before, she had little to do with that decision. I am determined to demonstrate my ability to maintain control over baser urges."

"Then we should probably avoid situations where we're going to lose our heads and do something we both might regret."

He could not argue that point, but he would have no regrets when it came to making love to her should they arrive upon that decision. He might regret any emotional entanglement. "I suppose you're correct, but chemistry is very hard to control."

"We'll just have to learn to control it for the time being."

Easier said than done. "And let us both hope we can maintain control."

"Believe me, you'll have enough distractions taking care of Sam."

Perhaps while caring for his son that would be true, but she served as his primary distraction in private, the reason why he began backing toward the door— and away from these foreign feelings for Piper that had little to do with physical attraction. "Speaking of my son, I should go see about him. In the meantime, you should rest."

She yawned again and stretched her arms above her head. "A nap would be fantastic. So would a shower. Is there one nearby?"

Old habits reared their ugly heads when he almost offered his personal facilities—and his assistance— but instead he nodded to his right. "You have an en suite bathroom through that door. And my room is right across the hall, should you find you require anything else from me."

Her grin returned. "I'm sure I'll manage, but thank you for everything."

"My pleasure, and I do hope you get some much-needed sleep filled with pleasant dreams."

No doubt he would be having a few pleasant—and inadvisable—dreams about her.

Four

At the sound of a crying baby, Piper awoke with a start. She tried to regain her bearings only to discover the room was too dark to see much of anything, leading her to fumble for the bedside lamp and snap it on.

Since she hadn't bothered to reset her watch after she showered, she didn't know the exact time, nor did she know how long she'd been sleeping. She did know that her once-damp hair had dislodged from the towel and her pink silk robe was practically wrapped around her neck.

After pushing off the bed, she immediately strode to the dresser to untangle her hair with a brush and to select appropriate clothing before setting off to see about Sam. But the continuous cries had her tightening the robe's sash as she left the room and plodded down the hall on bare feet.

She paused at the nursery to find the door ajar and a disheveled sheikh pacing the area, a very distressed son cradled in his arms. She strolled into the room, feeling slightly uneasy over her state of dress—or undress as the case might be. While she wore only a flimsy robe, he was dressed in a white T-shirt and faded jeans, his feet also bare. He looked tousled and sexy and, oh, so tempting…and she needed to shift her brain back into an appropriate gear. "Having problems?"

Adan paused the pacing to give her a forlorn look. "I have fed him twice and diapered him more times than I can possibly count, and he still continues to cry at the top of his lungs."

Taking pity on the prince, she walked up to him, took Sam from his grasp and began patting the baby's back. "Did you burp him?"

He lowered his gaze. "Actually, no, I did not."

"Then it's probably just a bubble in his tummy." She sat down in a nearby rocker, draped the baby horizontally over her knees and rubbed his back. "Did Talia happen to mention anything about colic?" she asked, and when he seemed confused, she launched into an explanation. "It's an odd occurrence that happens to some babies at the same time every night. Basically a stomachache that can't quite be explained. On a positive note, it eventually resolves itself, usually when they're around three months old."

He slid his hands into his pockets and approached her slowly. "I highly doubt Talia would have known if he had this problem. Are you certain it's not dangerous?"

He sounded so worried her heart went out to him. "No, it's not dangerous. But it's probably wise to have him checked out by a doctor as soon as possible, just to make sure he's healthy and growing at the right rate. And please tell me Talia left some sort of medical records with you."

"That much she did," he said. "My sister-in-law, who also happens to be the queen and head of our ministry of health, is a physician. I will have her examine Samuel as soon as she returns at the end of the week."

Although Sam's sobs had turned into sniffles, she continued to gently pat the baby's back in hopes of relieving his tummy distress. "It's good to have a doctor in the family. How do you think the king will take the news about Sam?"

Adan leaned a shoulder against the wall. "He is no stranger to scandal, so he has no reason to judge me."

She recalled reading a bit about that scandal during a pretravel internet search. "I remember seeing something about him marrying a divorced woman."

"Maysa is a remarkable woman," he said. "And say what you will about Rafiq's reputation for being rigid, at least he has been willing to bring the country into the twenty-first century. He had the elevator installed."

Piper thanked her lucky stars for that modern convenience. She also experienced more good fortune when the baby lifted his little head and let out a loud belch. "I believe Sam could use a warm bath now that his belly problem's solved. I can do it if you're too exhausted to take that on."

Finally, he smiled. "As long as you are there to guide me, I am a willing student."

Piper shifted Sam to her shoulder, pushed out of the chair and nodded toward the cupboard angled in the corner. "Elena said there are still some baby things in there. Take a look and see what we have available."

Adan strode to the large cabinet and opened the double doors, revealing shelves that housed numerous infant outfits and supplies. "If we do not have what we need here, then it does not exist."

She crossed the room to survey the bounty. "You could be right about that. And I see exactly what we need on the top shelf. Grab that blue tub and two towels. And next to that you'll see a small container with all the shampoo and stuff. Get that, too."

After Adan complied, he turned around, the bathing provisions balanced precariously in his arms. "Anything else?"

"Just show me to the sink and we'll bathe your little boy."

"In here," Adan said as he opened a door to his immediate right.

Piper stepped into the adjacent bath that was right out of an Arabian dream. The large double sink, with ornate gold fixtures, appeared to be made of copper. The shower to her left was composed of rich beige stones, much like the one in her guest suite, only she had access to a deep marble soaking tub. For a nursery she would deem it way over the top, but functional enough to bathe an infant.

"Lay the towels out on the vanity and put the tub in the sink," she instructed Adan. "Always make sure you have everything within reach."

"In case he climbs out of the bath?"

This time she laughed. "He won't, at least not at this age. Once he's too big for this setup, you'll bathe him in a regular tub."

He frowned. "I greatly look forward to that time."

"And it will be here before you know it." After he

had the supplies set out, she handed Sam to him. "Now lay him down and undress him while I test the water."

With the bath moderately filled and the baby undressed, she slid her hands beneath Sam and laid him gently in the tub. "You're on, Daddy."

Sam seemed to be thoroughly enjoying the process. His father—not so much. Yet Piper admired the care in which he bathed his son, though at times he seemed somewhat tentative, especially when it came to removing the infant from the tub.

"He's soaking wet," he said. "What if I drop him?"

In consideration of his inexperience, she picked up Sam beneath the arms, careful to support his head with her fingertips, and wrapped him securely in the hooded towel. "See how easy that was?"

"Easy for you," he said. "I will definitely need more practice."

"You'll definitely get that."

After carrying the baby back to the dressing table, Piper outfitted him in one-piece white footed pajamas. Sam was wide-eyed and more awake than she'd seen him to this point, and she automatically leaned over to kiss his cheek. "You're a happy baby now, aren't you, sweetie? You smell so good, too."

"And you are a natural mother, Piper McAdams."

She straightened to find Adan staring at her, a soft smile enhancing his gorgeous face. "I don't know about that, but I do love kids."

Without any prompting, he picked up his son and set him in the crook of his arm. "And I would say this lad is fairly taken with you. I cannot say that I blame him."

Piper felt heat rise to her face over the compliment and his nearness. "You're a great father, Adan. The two of you will make a good team for many, many years to come."

The pride in his expression was unmistakable. "I am determined to do my best by him. Yet I already sense bedtime could be an issue. He does not appear at all ready to sleep."

Piper checked the clock on the wall and noted the time at half past nine. "I had no idea it was that late. I slept through dinner."

He gestured toward the door. "By all means, return to your quarters and I will have a tray sent up."

She truly hated to leave him all alone on his first night as a father. "Are you sure? I'm really not that hungry." A patent lie. Sam's half-full bottle of formula set on the table was starting to look appetizing.

"I have to learn to do this by myself eventually," he said. "You need food and sleep to sustain you during our shopping trip tomorrow."

She sincerely looked forward to the outing. "All right, but please let me know if you need help with Sam at any point during the night."

He reached over and pushed a damp strand of hair from her cheek. "You have done more than your share, Piper. I cannot express how much I appreciate your guidance."

He had no idea how much she appreciated his willingness to take on raising a baby on his own. "It was my pleasure. And before I turn in for the night, I'll make a list of things you'll need for the baby."

He grinned, showing his dimples to full advantage. "Perhaps I should purchase a pack mule while we're out."

She shrugged. "As long as you don't mind showing your ass all over town."

His laugh was gruff and extremely sexy. "I would rather show my son off all over town, so we will forgo the mule for the moment."

Piper wanted to argue against creating too much attention to his newly discovered child, but Adan seemed so proud of Sam, she didn't dare discourage him. In twenty-six years, her own mother had never expressed that devotion, nor would she ever.

Besides, the possibility of another scandal would fall on the royal family's shoulders, and they'd most likely dealt with those issues before. And if they played their cards right, no one would discover the prince in disguise in their midst.

Piper would swear the store clerk had recognized Adan, even though he wore a New York Yankees baseball cap covering his dark hair, sunglasses covering his amber eyes, khaki cargo pants, black T-shirt and heavy boots. Not to mention he hadn't shaved that morning, evident by the light blanket of whiskers along his chin, upper lip and jaw. She definitely liked that rugged, manly look. A lot. And maybe that was what had garnered the young woman's attention—Adan's sheer animal magnetism.

Yes, that had to be it. Why else would she giggle when Adan leaned over the counter and handed her the supply list? Unfortunately Piper couldn't understand a word they were saying, which left her to guess. And she'd begun to assume the sheikh might be making a date.

The baby began to stir in the stroller they'd pur-

chased on their first stop, drawing Piper's attention and
giving her a valid excuse to interrupt the exchange. "I
believe Sam is going to want a bottle very soon."

He pushed away from the counter and glanced at
Sam, who looked as if he might be in precrying mode.
"I believe you are correct. We should be finished here
soon."

After Adan spoke to the clerk again, she disappeared
into a back room and returned a few moments later with
a scowling, middle-aged man carrying three cardboard
boxes. He set the boxes down hard on the counter, then
eyed Adan suspiciously before he sent Piper a clear look
of contempt. She had no idea what they had done to
warrant his disdain, but she was relieved when he disappeared into the back area again. After the young woman
placed the clothing, toys and other provisions they'd se-
lected into several bags, Adan counted out cash—a lot
of cash—then smiled when his admirer fumbled with
the receipt before she finally set it in his open palm.

Ready for a quick escape before the love-struck clerk
fainted, Piper flipped her sunglasses back into place—
and immediately saw a problem with transporting the
items since the driver had parked in an alley two blocks
away to avoid detection. "Looks like we're going to
have to make several trips to get all of this to the car."

"I'll take care of that," Adan replied as he headed
out the exit, leaving her behind with a fussy baby and
a smitten cashier.

Piper could easily remedy one problem by giving
Sam a bottle. While she was rummaging through the
diaper bag to do that very thing, she noticed the grumpy
guy standing behind the counter, staring at her. She
immediately glanced down to make sure the sundress

hadn't slipped down and exposed too much cleavage. Not the case at all. And when she scooped the baby from the stroller to feed him, he continued to look at her as if she was a scourge on society.

Fortunately Adan returned a few moments later, three teenage boys dressed in muslin tunics and pants trailing behind him. He handed them each a few bills, barked a few orders, and like a well-oiled human machine, the trio picked up the supplies, awaiting further instruction.

After opening the door, Adan made a sweeping gesture with one hand. "After you, fair lady."

"Thank you, kind sir, and please bring the stroller and the bag."

With Sam in her arms and the secret sheikh by her side, they stepped onto the stone sidewalk and traveled past clay-colored artisan shops and small eateries. The luscious scents of a nearby restaurant reminded Piper they hadn't yet had lunch. The way people stared at them reminded her of the overly stern guy in the store. "Did you notice how that older man in the boutique kept looking at us?" she asked Adan as she handed him the empty bottle, then brought Sam up to her shoulder.

He dropped the bottle back into the bag resting in the stroller without breaking his stride. "Some of Bajul's citizens are not particularly fond of foreigners."

That made sense. Sort of. "He actually seemed angry."

"Perhaps he noticed you were not wearing a ring and assumed we are unmarried with a child."

"He would be wrong on all counts."

Piper experienced a sudden melancholy over that fact. She'd learned long ago not to chase unattainable dreams, and wanting more from Adan would definitely qualify. She still wasn't sure she could entirely trust him, although he seemed to be making an effort to earn it. Even so, she was clearly in danger of becoming too close to the baby—and the baby's father.

As they rounded the corner and entered the alley, a series of shouts startled the sleeping baby awake. Sam began to cry and Piper began to panic when a crowd of people converged upon them on the way to the car. Most members of the press, she surmised when she noticed the microphones being thrust in Adan's face. She hadn't been able to understand the questions until one lanky blond English-speaking reporter stepped forward. "Whose child is this, Sheikh Mehdi?"

Overcome with the need to protect Adan, Piper responded without thought. "He's mine."

She managed to open the car door as the driver loaded the trunk, escaping the chaos. But she'd barely settled inside before the reporter blocked the prince's path. "Is the baby your bastard child?"

Adan grabbed the journalist by the collar with both hands. "The child is not a bastard," he hissed. "He is my son."

Piper saw a disaster in the making and had to intervene. "Adan, he's not worth it."

The reporter cut a look in her direction. "Is this woman your mistress?"

Adan pointed in her direction. "That woman is… She is…my wife."

"*Your wife?* What were you thinking, Adan?"

He hadn't been thinking at all, only reacting. But after spending a good hour sitting on the veranda outside the nursery, that was all he had been doing. "The bloody imbecile insulted my child, and then he insulted you."

Piper yanked the chair opposite his back from the table and sat. "Telling the press we're married was a bit extreme, don't you agree?"

That extreme stemmed from wrath over the circumstance. "Had you not begun this debacle by claiming to be Samuel's mother, then I would not have had to defend yours and my son's honor."

She sent him a withering look. "For your information, I was simply trying to protect you from answering questions you weren't prepared to answer. I had no idea you were going tell the world you're Sam's father, nor did I have a clue you were going to have us living in wedded bliss."

"I believe that would be preferable to confirming you're nothing more than a mistress who bore my *bastard* child."

"What would have been wrong with letting everyone believe he's mine and leave it at that?"

His anger returned with the strength of a tempest. "I will not deny my son to anyone. Under any circumstance."

She blew an upward breath that ruffled her bangs. "Okay, it's obvious we're not going to get anywhere by playing the blame game. The question is, what are you going to do now? I don't think moving to Antarctica is a viable option with a month-old child."

The trip was beginning to appeal to him greatly. "If I refuse to comment further, the rumors will eventually die down."

She leaned back and released an acerbic laugh. "By the time Sam turns twenty?"

He recognized the absurdity in believing any scandal involving the Mehdi family would simply go away. "You're right. I will have to come up with some way to explain the situation. But I will not retract my statement regarding my son."

She appeared resigned. "I understand that, but you have to be worried Talia might find out someone else is pretending to be your son's mother, not to mention your wife. If she decides to come forward, everyone will know Sam's the result of a relationship out of wedlock and you lied about our marriage."

Since his ex was the consummate publicity hound, handing her that bone could prove to be problematic eventually. "To my good fortune, she's unreachable at the moment. I highly doubt she will hear any of this until she returns to France."

"Possibly, but I'm sure the king has heard by now and—" she streaked both hands down her face "—if my grandfather finds out, he'll demand I board the next plane bound for the Carolinas."

Despite what had transpired an hour ago, he still did not want her to leave for many reasons. "As far as I know, you have not yet been identified."

"I saw camera flashes."

"And you were wearing sunglasses. You could be any number of women who've crossed my path." He regretted the comment the moment it left his stupid mouth.

"All your ex-lovers?" she asked, her voice surprisingly calm.

He grasped for anything to dig himself out of the hole. "I meant any woman, whether I've slept with her or not. When you are constantly in the spotlight, your reputation becomes completely overblown. My brother Zain could attest to that. His reputation preceded him before he married Madison."

"I recall Elena mentioning they're in Los Angeles," she said. "Is his wife from the States?"

"Yes, and she is unequivocally the best thing that has ever happened to him. I sincerely never believed he would settle down with one woman."

She leaned back against the seat and began to toy with the diamond pendant dangling between her breasts. "Well, since I'm apparently just any woman, I suppose I shouldn't be worried at all. However, if I know the press, it's only a matter of time before they learn who I am."

Adan pushed out of the chair and moved to the veranda's edge to stare at the mountainous panorama he had always taken for granted. "It would be better for Samuel if everyone believed you are his mother, not Talia. She has quite a few skeletons in her dressing room closet."

Piper joined him and folded her arms atop the ledge. "Haven't we all in some way?"

He turned and leaned back against the stone wall. "I would have a difficult time believing you have anything scandalous to hide."

She smiled. "Well, apparently I gave birth and I haven't been exposed to sex in quite some time. That would be some fairly heavy fodder for the gossipmongers."

He shook his head and returned her smile. "It's good to see your wit is still intact."

"Hey, if you can't immediately fix a terrible situation, you might as well find some humor in it."

A true optimist. He added that to his ever-expanding

list of her attributes. "Do you consider the thought of being wed to me so terrible?"

"Actually, I can think of a few perks being married to you would provide."

He inched closer to her. "What perks do you have in mind?"

She faced him and folded her arms beneath her breasts. "Living in a palace immediately comes to mind."

Not at all what he'd wanted to hear. "That's it?"

"Who wouldn't want to be waited on hand and foot?"

He reached out and tucked her hair behind her ear. "I'm disappointed that's the best you can do."

She frowned. "If you want me to include your expertise as a lover, I can't speak to that because I don't know. Not that I didn't try my best to convince you to show me in your hotel room."

He still wanted to be her lover. More than he'd wanted anything in quite some time, aside from being a worthy father to his son. "Since the rest of the world now believes we've conceived a child together, perhaps we should give lovemaking serious consideration."

Her grin rivaled the sun setting on the horizon. "Procreation in reverse. I kind of like the thought of that, but..." Her words trailed off along with her gaze.

"You still doubt my honor." He hadn't been able to mask the disappointment in his tone.

"You're wrong," she said adamantly. "I realize now only an honorable man would so obviously love a child he just met. I see it every time you look at Sam."

Every time he looked at her, he felt things he could not explain, and shouldn't be feeling. "Then what would stop you from exploring our relationship on an intimate level, particularly when you were so bent on doing so in Chicago?"

"I'm taking your need for celibacy into consideration."

That vow was quickly becoming the bane of his existence. "I do not believe that to be the case."

She sighed. "Fine. Truth is, I don't want to get hurt."

He slid a fingertip along her jaw. "I would never do anything to hurt you, Piper."

"Not intentionally," she said. "But if we take that all-important step, I worry it's going to be too hard to walk away. And we both know I'll be walking away sooner than later."

Letting her walk away wouldn't be one of his finest moments, either. But he could make no promises. "I propose we continue with our original plan and learn all we can about each other while you're here. Anything beyond that will happen only if we mutually decide it's beneficial for both of us."

She tapped her chin and pretended to think. "A prince with benefits. That does sound intriguing."

He had resisted her long enough was his last thought before he reeled her into his arms and kissed her. She didn't reject the gesture at all. She didn't push him away or tense against him. She simply kissed him back like a woman who had not been kissed enough. And as usual, his body responded in a way that would merit a serious scolding from his former governess.

Bent on telling her what she was doing to him, he brought his lips to her ear. "If we had no care in the world, and all the privacy we needed, I would lift up your dress, lower your panties and take you right here."

She pulled back and stared at him with hazy eyes. "I could think of worse things."

He could think of something much better. "You deserve a bed and champagne and candles our first time."

"You're certainly not lacking in confidence."

Subtlety had never been his strongest suit. "Provided we decide to take that next step."

"Provided we could actually find the time to do it while adhering to your son's schedule."

Right on time, the sound of a crying baby filtered out through the nursery's open window. "I shall go see about him," he said without removing his hold or his gaze from her.

"I'll do it," she answered without making a single move.

"I already have."

Adan glanced to his right to see Elena strolling onto the terrace, his son in her arms, sending him away from Piper. "We were on our way."

Elena rolled her eyes. "You were on your way, all right, but that had nothing to do with the *bambino*."

Caught by the former nanny like a juvenile delinquent stealing candy from the market. "We shall take charge of him now."

Elena moved in front of him and smiled. "I will watch him for a while until you and Miss McAdams return."

"Where are we going?" Piper asked before he could respond.

"Your presence is requested in the conference room. Both of you."

Perhaps the first information from the engineers, although he had a difficult time believing they'd have anything significant to report in such a short time. "Shouldn't we wait to meet with the conservation crew until after Rafiq returns?"

"Rafiq arrived a few minutes ago," Elena said. "He called the meeting."

Damn it all to hell. He'd been summoned to take his place in the king's hot seat. "Did he happen to mention anything about water conservation?"

"I would speculate he's interested in conserving the military commander in chief's reputation." Elena cradled the baby closer and patted Adan's arm. "Good luck, *cara.* You are absolutely going to need it."

Depending on what his brother had in store for him, he could very well need to call out the royal guard.

Five

Dead silence—Piper's first impression the minute she followed Adan into the conference room for the so-called meeting. And she had no doubt she knew exactly what was on the agenda—quite possibly her head delivered to her personally by the king of Bajul.

He wore a black silk suit, dark gray tie and a definite air of authority. His coal-colored eyes and near-black hair would qualify him as darkly handsome, and somewhat intimidating. *Very* intimidating, Piper realized when he pushed back from the head of the mahogany table and came to his feet. Adan might be an inch or so taller, but his brother's aura of sheer power made him seem gigantic.

The mysterious Mr. Deeb stood nearby, absently studying his glasses before he repositioned them over his eyes. "Please join us," he said, indicating the two chairs on each side of the stoic monarch.

Adan had already settled in before Piper had gathered enough courage to walk forward. She could do this. She could face Rafiq Mehdi with a calm head and feigned confidence. Or she could turn and run.

Choosing the first option for diplomacy's sake, she claimed the chair opposite Adan as the king sat and folded his hands before him on the tabletop. "It is a pleasure to meet you, Ms. McAdams," he began, "though I would have preferred to have done so under different circumstances."

She would have preferred not to meet him at all today, if ever. Sucking up seemed like a fantastic idea. "The pleasure is all mine, Your Excellency. My grandfather has said some wonderful things about your leadership. And you may call me Piper."

"And you may address me as Rafiq, since it seems you have become a part of the royal family without my knowledge."

Piper swallowed hard around her chagrin. "Actually, that's not—"

"Are you going to jump to conclusions without hearing our side of the story, Rafiq?" Adan asked, a serious hint of impatience in his tone.

The king leaned back and studied them both for a moment. "I am giving you the opportunity now."

"I have a son," Adan said. "That whole wife issue was simply a misunderstanding, and that is all there is to the story."

Rafiq released a gruff laugh. "I fear you are wrong about that, brother. I know this because I have heard the entire sordid tale. And I do believe that included you delivering the 'wife' proclamation yourself."

Piper noticed an immediate change in Adan's demeanor. He definitely didn't appear quite as confident as he had when they'd entered the room. She had to come to his defense due to her contribution to the mess. "Your Excellency, I'm in part responsible for—"

Adan put up a hand to silence her. "It was simply an error in judgment on both our parts. We were attempting to protect each other and my son."

"Yet instead you have created a scandal at a time when we are trying to convince our people this conservation project is worthwhile," Rafiq replied. "Their attention has now been diverted from the need to relocate some of the farms to an illegitimate child born to the man in charge of protecting our borders."

"Never use that word to describe my son again," Adan hissed. "I may not have known about him, but he is every bit a Mehdi."

Rafiq looked extremely surprised. "I never thought of you as being the paternal sort, Adan. That being said, it is my understanding his true mother is the narcissistic Talia Thorpe."

Evidently the royal family and staff held the model in very low esteem. "That's true," Piper interjected before she could be cut off again. "I was simply pretending to be the baby's mother to delay the questions over his parentage."

"Yet everyone now believes you are his mother," Rafiq replied. "That has created quite the dilemma."

"I promise you I will handle this," Adan said. "I will retract the marriage statement and explain that Samuel is my child from a previous relationship."

Rafiq straightened and scowled. "You will do no such thing."

Adan exchanged a look with Piper before bringing his attention back to his brother. "You would have us continue the lie?"

"As a matter of fact, that is exactly what you will do," Rafiq began, "until you find some way to be rid of the model, for both yours and your heir's sake. Naming her as the mother will only wreak more havoc. The woman is known for posing in the nude in several photographs."

The king's condescension ruffled Piper's artistic feathers. "Some do not find nudity offensive. It would depend on what the photographer was attempting to convey."

"Centerfold photos," Adan added. "She posed for several magazines, in print and online. Some of those publications are obscure and questionable at best."

That did change everything from an artistic standpoint. "Are they widely circulated here?"

Adan looked somewhat sheepish. "After word got out that we were involved."

The king turned his full attention to her. "Ms. McAdams, if you would kindly continue the charade until your departure, then we will make certain you are compensated."

She could not believe someone was offering to pay her for a humongous fib that could alter her own life. "No offense, Your Excellency, but I can't in good conscience accept money for my silence."

"Temporary silence," the king added. "And I was not suggesting a bribe. However, I will award the contract to your corporation upon review of the bid. Once you have returned to the States, we will issue a statement saying you felt it best that the marriage be dissolved on the basis of irreconcilable differences, and that you feel your son should live in his homeland."

"And what do you propose we do with Talia?" Adan asked. "Bind and gag her before she leaks the truth to the media?"

"*She* we will have to pay," Rafiq stated. "I am certain it will cost a fortune to have her relinquish her rights as well as execute a legal document forbidding her to have any claim on the child. Fortunately, you have the means to meet her price, however high that might be."

Adan released a weary sigh. "Rafiq, this could all backfire no matter how carefully we plan. Talia could refuse to meet our terms, and furthermore, the truth may surface no matter how hard we try to conceal it."

"I trust that you and Ms. McAdams will see that does not happen."

The man was making too many impossible demands as far as Piper was concerned. "How do you propose we do that when you risk someone within these walls leaking that information?"

"The staff normally practices absolute discretion," Rafiq said, mirroring Adan's words from the day they discovered Sam existed. "Yet it would be foolish not to believe someone with lesser responsibility in the palace could sell the information to the highest bidder. Therefore it is paramount you both act as if you are a wedded couple at all times. We will issue a press release stating you were married at an undisclosed location prior to the pregnancy."

As she regarded Adan, Piper couldn't quite contain her sarcasm. "Would that be all right with you, dear?"

He shook his head. "None of this is right, but I do believe it is a viable plan, at least for the time being."

She saw her control over the situation begin to slip away. "Do I have any say in the matter?"

"Yes you do," Rafiq said. "You are free to refuse and leave immediately. With your company's crew."

A not-so-veiled threat. She mulled over a laundry list of pros and cons while Adan and the king waited for her answer. If she didn't agree, they would lose the contract, and that could send the struggling business into a free fall. If she did agree, she would have to stay on for at least a month immersed in a massive lie. And most important, she would be charged with contacting her grandparents to break the news before someone else did. She could only imagine her grandfather's reaction to either scenario. Then again, if she went along with the marriage pretense, she'd have the opportunity to stand up to him once and for all if he gave her any grief. She could finally be her own person and control her own life—for at least a month. Not a bad thing, at that.

A few more seconds ticked off while she weighed her options. The one bright spot she could see coming out of this entire debacle had directly to do with Adan. Being his make-believe spouse could come with some serious perks.

She drew in a deep breath, let it out slowly and said, "I'll do it."

Adan looked caught completely off guard. "You will?"

"I will." She rose from the chair and managed a smile. "Now, if you gentlemen would please excuse me, this pretend wife needs to make a call to her very real grandparents."

Adan stood and returned her smile. "Feel free to use my private study next door."

"Thanks. I believe I will."

Piper did an about-face, strode into the hall and prepared to lie.

"Have you totally lost your ever-lovin' mind, sweet pea?"

Oh, how she hated her grandfather's pet name for her. But Piper had to admit she was enjoying his shock. She'd never seriously shocked anyone in her sheltered life up to this point, at least not to this extreme. "No, Poppa, I'm quite sane. I would have told you sooner about the marriage but it was rather spontaneous." And pure fiction.

"When did you meet this character?"

Lie number one. "Quite a while ago, when I was in the U.K. last year."

"And you didn't bother to tell me this when you knew full well I was sending you to his country? That dog just don't hunt."

Lie number two. "We've kept our relationship quiet because we didn't want other contractors thinking I could influence the bidding process."

"And you don't have an influence over the bid now that you've gotten yourself hitched to him, sweet pea?"

Lie number three. "Not at all."

A span of silence passed before he responded. "I guess there's nothing I can do about it now, but at least it's good to know he's got royal blood and money to burn."

Of course that would be Walter McAdams's main concern when it came to her choice in a life partner. It always had been. "I'm sure when you met him back in Chicago you realized he's a very charming man."

"A charming snake," he muttered. "Of course, your grandmother's all atwitter over this. She wants to talk to you, so hang on a minute."

Piper heard him put down the receiver, followed by muffled conversation before someone picked up the phone again. "My little sugar plum is a married woman!"

Enough with the overly sweet endearments, she wanted to say, but kept her impatience in check. "Yes, Nana, I finally took the plunge." Headlong into a humongous fabricated fairy tale.

"I saw a picture of him on the internet, Piper. My, my, he's a good-looking young man. When did you two meet?"

Piper was frankly sick to death of fibbing, so she decided to try on the truth. "In a hotel bar. I attempted to seduce him but he didn't take the bait. He's quite the gentleman."

As usual, her grandmother giggled like a schoolgirl, a good indicator she didn't believe what she'd heard. "Oh, child, you are still such a cutup when it comes to boys. And you don't have to tell me any details right now."

But she did have to tell her more truths. "Nana, Adan is a very public figure, so you might hear a few rumors that aren't exactly accurate."

"What kind of rumors?" she asked with obvious concern.

She could trust her grandmother with some of the facts, even if the woman was a little too steeped in Southern society. "First, you have to promise me that whatever I tell you, it has to remain strictly confidential."

"Sugar, you know how I abhor gossip."

An advantage for Piper in this gossip game. "All right. You're probably going to hear that we've had a baby together."

Nana released an audible gasp. "Did you?"

Heavens, the woman wasn't thinking straight. "Do you recall me even remotely looking pregnant over the past few months?"

"Well, no."

"Precisely, because I wasn't. Adan does have an infant son, but obviously I'm not his mother. That said, as far as the world knows, Samuel is my baby. The biological mother's identity is a well-kept secret and has to remain so for reasons I can't reveal."

"Is she an actress? Maybe a singer? Oh, wait. Is she a call girl?"

Piper had no idea Drusilla McAdams even knew what that was. "Don't worry about it. I just need you to refuse to comment on anything if any reporters track you and Poppa down, and keep everything I've told you to yourself. Can you do that, Nana?"

"I certainly can, sugar plum," she said. "And I'm so proud of you, sweetie. It's admirable you're willing to take another woman's child and raise it as your own."

"I learned that from you, Nana."

A span of silence passed before her grandmother spoke again. "I have never regretted raising you and your sister, Piper. I do regret that Millie could never be a decent mother to you. But that's mine and your Poppa's fault. We spoiled her too much, maybe even loved her too much. She never had a care in the world aside from herself."

She still didn't as far as Piper could tell. She'd barely even seen her fly-by-night mother over the past few years, let alone established a relationship with her. "You were very good to me and Sunny, Nana. Millie is responsible for her behavior, not you. And I don't believe you can ever love anyone too much."

"Only if they can't possibly love you back, honey."

Her grandmother's words gave her some cause for concern. If she happened to stupidly fall in love with Adan, she wondered if he had the capacity to return her feelings. Probably not, and she certainly didn't intend to find out. Sadly, sometimes intentions went awry. "Look, Nana, I have a few things to do, but first, do you have any questions for me?" Piper held her breath and hoped for a no.

"Yes I do. How is the sheikh when it comes to… you know?"

Regretfully Piper hadn't experienced "you know"… yet. "Nana, a girl's gotta have her secrets, so I'll only say I'm not at all disappointed." Should she and Adan take that lovemaking step, she would wager she wouldn't be disappointed in the least.

"That's a good thing, sugar plum. What goes on between the sheets better be good if you want to sustain a relationship. Your grandfather and I have been happily going after—"

"I'd better go." Before they wandered into too-much-information territory. "I'll talk to you both real soon."

"Okay, but your grandfather told me to deliver a message before you hang up, the old grump."

Lovely. "What is it?"

"Married or not, you still have a job to do, and he expects a full report on the survey crew's progress within the next two days."

So much for spending time with father and son. For the time being, Adan would just have to go it alone.

"Congratulations, Dad. Your baby is the picture of health."

Adan turned from the crib to face Maysa Barad Mehdi—Arabian beauty, American-educated premiere physician and current queen of Bajul. "Are you absolutely certain? He seems rather small to me."

His sister-in-law sent him a sympathetic look, much to his chagrin. "He's not quite five weeks old, Adan, so he's going to be small. Fortunately Ms. Thorpe had the foresight to include copies of his medical records since his birth. He's gaining weight at a favorable pace and I expect that to continue." She paused and sent him a smile. "And before you know it, he will have a playmate."

Clearly the woman had taken leave of her senses. "I have no intention of having another child in the near future, if ever." First, he would have to have a willing partner, and his thoughts immediately turned to Piper. With her he wouldn't be seeking procreation, only practice. As much practice as she would allow, if she allowed any at all after being thrust into Rafiq's harebrained scheme.

"Let me rephrase that," Maysa said. "Samuel will have a new cousin in a little less than eight months."

Adan let that sink in for a moment before he responded, "You're pregnant?"

"Yes, I am."

He gave her a fond embrace. "Congratulations to you, as well. How is Rafiq handling impending parenthood?"

Her expression turned somber. "He is worried to death, though he tries not to show it."

"That's understandable considering the accident." The freak car accident that had claimed Rafiq's former wife and unborn child. A horrific event that had turned his brother into a temporary tyrant. "I'm certain he will relax eventually."

She frowned. "Did you only recently meet Rafiq, Adan? The man does not know the first thing about relaxing. I only hope he calms somewhat before the birth. Otherwise we'll have a fretful child."

He couldn't imagine Rafiq remaining calm under such a stressful situation. "Perhaps having Samuel around will demonstrate that tending to an infant isn't rocket science. If I can manage it, then certainly so will he."

She patted his cheek. "And you are doing very well from what I hear."

Curiosity and concern drove him to ask, "What else have you heard?"

"If you're wondering if I know about the presumed marriage, I do. My husband told me you could not have chosen a more suitable counterfeit wife." She accentuated the barb with a grin.

He found little humor in the current state of affairs. "This entire situation reeks of fraud, and I find it appalling that I've drawn Piper into that web of deceit. She's a remarkable woman and deserves much better."

Maysa inclined her head and studied him a few moments. "You sound as if you care a great deal for her."

More than he would ever let on—to Piper or to himself. "I've only known her a few days, yet I admittedly like what I do know."

"It shows," she said. "Your face lights up at the mention of her name."

A complete exaggeration. "Women always seem to imagine things that aren't there," he muttered. "Just because I am fond of her does not mean I see her as anything other than my unwitting partner in crime." But he could see her as his lover, as he had often in his fantasies. "I certainly have no plans to make this marriage real."

"We'll see," Maysa said as she covered the now-sleeping infant with the blanket. "One never knows what will transpire once intimacy is involved."

"I am not sleeping with her, Maysa," he said, a little too defensively. "And as it stands now, that is not on the to-do list." At least not on the one he wasn't hiding.

Maysa flipped a lock of her waist-length hair over one shoulder. "Adan, when you do not have an agenda that includes bedding a woman, then the world has truly spun on its axis."

If he had his way, someday people would see him as more than a womanizer. They would see him as a good father. "As always, dear queen, you are correct, at least partially. I would be telling a tale if I said I had not considered consummating our relationship. She's beautiful and intelligent and possesses a keen wit. She is also in many ways an innocent. For that reason I have vowed not to take advantage of her trusting nature."

"Perhaps you should explore the possibilities," she said. "And I do not mean in a sexual sense. You should take this time to get to know her better. You might be pleasantly surprised at what you learn."

Exactly as he had promised both himself and Piper— getting to know each other better before they took the next step. That was before he'd learned he had a son. "I see several problems with that prospect. Being charged with Samuel's care is taxing and time-consuming. Commanding the whole bloody Royal Air Force doesn't require as much attention."

Maysa began returning supplies to her black doctor's bag resting on the dressing table where she'd performed the examination on his son. "Then perhaps you will be happy to know my husband has instructed me to tell you to take your bride away for two days for a respite."

Adan firmly believed his brother had taken leave of his senses. "Why would he suggest that?"

She snapped the bag closed and turned toward him. "He's trying to buy more time, Adan. The media have already been hounding him for an interview with you, and it will only become worse once the palace releases an official statement later today. Rafiq feels that if he tells them you're away for a brief holiday, they'll let up for the time being. And considering Samuel's age, this would be the appropriate time for you to resume your husbandly duty."

He could not resume a duty he had yet to undertake. However, the prospect of spending more time with his presumed wife was greatly appealing, yet he could not ignore the obvious issues. "I cannot abandon Samuel."

"I am sure Elena would wholeheartedly step in while you're gone."

"Actually, she wouldn't," he said. "She's made it quite clear that she is handing all the responsibility to me."

"Then I will watch him until you return. And you are more than welcome to take your new wife to the resort."

He had his own secluded resort equipped with a pool where they could spend some quality time. Then again, swimming with Piper would involve very little clothing. Not a good scenario for a man who for months had engaged in sexual deprivation in order to build character. At the moment, he had enough character to rival philanthropists worldwide. "I certainly appreciate your offer, but I would not want to burden you with my responsibility."

"It's not a burden at all," Maysa said as she leaned over and touched the top of Samuel's head. "I consider it an opportunity to practice parenthood. Now, hurry along while you still have the better part of the day."

A plan began to formulate in Adan's brain. A good plan involving his favorite mode of transportation. Now all he had to do was convince Piper to come along for the ride of her life.

After the harrowing trip to the airbase, Piper would be out of her mind if she agreed to go on this little flying excursion in the miniplane built for two. "You don't really believe I'm going to climb into that sardine can, do you?"

Adan flipped his aviators up to rest atop his head and tried to grin his way out of trouble, which wasn't going to work on Piper. Much. "This happens to be a very solid aircraft," he said.

Solid, maybe. Too tiny. Definitely. "First, you make me wear a massive helmet, throw me onto the back of a motorcycle and travel at excessive speeds on skinny little back roads to get here—"

"That was designed to evade the press, and if my memory serves me correctly, you came along willingly."

Darn it, she had. "That's not the point. Now you want me to get into a plane equivalent to a golf cart with wings."

He moved in front of said wing and patted the white plane's belly as if it were a favored pet. "Do not let the propeller scare you away. This is a Royal Air Force training craft meticulously maintained by our best mechanics. And of course, you are in good hands with me as your personal pilot."

A personal pilot with great hands, and she sure would like to know how they would feel all over her body. Maybe today she might actually find out. Maybe squeezing into this plane would be well worth it. "Just show me to my seat."

He grinned and opened the miniature door. "Hand over your bag and I will assist you."

Piper relinquished the tote to Adan, as well as her coveted control. "Here you are, and be careful with it because it contains some breakable items."

His smile melted into a scowl. "This bag must weigh ten pounds. Did you pack all your worldly belongings?"

She playfully slapped at his biceps, well aware he had one heck of a muscle. "No, I did not. I just packed a swimsuit and a change of clothes, per your request. I also brought along a few toiletries and sunscreen and towels. And a small sketch pad and pencils, in case I want to immortalize our day together on paper."

His smile returned full force. "It is quite possible you will not have time to sketch."

That sounded very promising. "And why would that be, Your Highness?"

He leaned over and brushed a kiss across her cheek. "Well, my pretend princess, I have several activities planned to occupy our time."

She could think of only one activity at the moment that interested her. "Can you give me a hint?"

"No. I want you to be surprised." He executed a slight bow. "Now climb into my chariot, fair lady, and we will begin our adventure."

She managed a not-half-bad curtsy. "As you wish, good sir."

Luckily the step up into the two-seater plane wasn't all that steep, but the small space seemed somewhat claustrophobic once Adan took his place beside her.

After strapping himself in, he handed her a headset. "Put this on and we'll be able to hear each other over the engine noise."

Noisy engine—not good. "Are you sure this is safe?" she asked before she covered her ears.

"Positive. And don't look so worried. We'll barely be off the ground before it's time to land again."

"A planned landing, I hope," she muttered as she adjusted the bulky headphones.

From that point forward, Piper watched Adan in action as he guided the pitiful excuse for a plane to the airstrip adjacent to the fleet of high-powered jets. As he did a final check, the Arabic exchange between Adan and the air traffic controller sounded like gibberish to her. But once he began to taxi down the runway, she didn't care if the pilot was speaking pig Latin. She held her breath, fisted her hands in her lap, gritted her teeth and closed her eyes tightly.

During liftoff, her stomach dipped as if she were riding a roller coaster. She felt every bump and sway as they gained altitude, and even when the plane seemed to level off, she still refused to look.

"You are missing some incredible scenery."

Feeling somewhat foolish, Piper forced herself to peer out the window at the terrain now cast in the midmorning sun. She noticed only a few man-made structures dotting the landscape, but the approaching mountains looked as if she could reach out and touch them, and that did nothing for her anxiety.

As if sensing her stress, Adan reached over the controls and took her hand. "This is the best view of my country," he said. "And when I am flying, I feel completely at peace."

She wished she could say the same for herself. "I've got a swarm of butterflies in my belly."

"I had no idea you're such a nervous flier."

"Not usually," she said. "I've never been in an aircraft quite this small before."

"Try to think of this as being as close to heaven as you can possibly be."

"I'd prefer not to get too much closer."

He grinned and squeezed her hand. "I will have you earthbound in a matter of minutes. If you look straight ahead, you'll see where we are going to land."

She tried to focus on the horizon, and not the descent toward the ground. Or the fact Adan was guiding them toward what appeared to be no more than a glorified dirt road—and a rather large mountain not far away. Her stomach dipped along with the plane as they approached the makeshift runway, but this time she kept her eyes open. She still remained as tense as a tightrope when the wheels touched down and they bounced a time or two before coming to a stop.

Piper let out the breath she'd been holding and looked around to find a thick copse of odd-looking trees surrounding them, but no signs of human life. "Where are we?"

Adan removed his headset, then hers, and smiled. "I am about to show you my most favorite place on the planet, and an experience you will not soon forget."

Six

"Wow."

Piper's wide-eyed reaction to the mountain retreat greatly pleased Adan. He'd brought only one other woman there, and she'd complained incessantly about the lack of facilities. But then Talia wasn't fond of sacrificing creature comforts for nature's bounty.

"It's basically a simple structure," he explained as he led her farther into the lone living area. "It's comprised of native wood and powered by solar energy. The water comes from the nearby lake to the house through a filtering system."

She walked to the sofa and ran her fingertips along the back of the black leather cushion. "It's very comfortable and cozy."

Her code for small, he surmised. "It has all one would require in this setting. One loft bedroom and a bath upstairs, another bedroom and bath downstairs, and my study."

She turned and smiled. "No kitchen?"

He pointed to his left. "Behind the stone wall, and it's the most impressive part of the house. However, I rarely utilize the stove, but I do make good use of the refrigerator and microwave."

"No housekeeper available?"

"No, but I do have a caretaker. He and his wife look after the place when I'm away."

She dropped down onto the beige club chair and curled her legs beneath her. "What possessed you to build a place out in the middle of nowhere?"

"You will soon see." After setting her bag on the bamboo floor, Adan crossed the room and pushed aside the drapes, revealing the mountainous terrain.

"Wow again," Piper said as she came to his side. "A view and your own private pool. I'm impressed."

He slid double doors open, bringing the outdoors inside. "This greatly expands the living space. And you'll appreciate the scenery far better from the veranda."

She smiled. "Then lead the way."

When Piper followed him onto the deck containing an outdoor kitchen and several tables with matching chairs, Adan paused at the top of the steps leading to the infinity pool. "This glorified bathtub took two years to build."

"It's absolutely incredible."

So was this woman beside him. He sat on the first step and signaled her to join him. Once she complied, he attempted not to notice the way her white shorts rode up her thighs, or the cleavage showing from the rounded neck in her sleeveless coral top that formed to her breasts very nicely. "This has always been my sanctuary of sorts. A good place to escape."

She took her attention from the water and turned it on him. "Exactly what are you escaping, Adan?"

He'd asked himself that question many times, and the answers were always the same. "I suppose the drudgery of being a royal. Perhaps the responsibility of overseeing an entire military operation. At one time, my father."

The final comment brought about her frown. "Was he that hard on you?"

He sighed. "No. He wasn't particularly concerned with what I did. I once believed he'd never quite recovered from losing my mother." That was before he'd learned his father's secrets.

"You mentioned your mother when we were in Chicago," she began, "but you didn't say what happened to her. Of course, if it makes you uncomfortable to talk about it, I understand."

Oddly, he wanted to tell her about his mother, what little he knew of Cala Mehdi. He wanted to tell her many things he'd never spoken of to anyone. And eventually he would tell her their visit would be extended beyond the afternoon. "Her death was a mystery of sorts. She was found at the bottom of the mountain near the lake. Most believed she'd taken a fall. Some still wonder if she'd taken her own life due to depression following my birth. I've accepted the fact I'll never know the truth."

"Are you sure you've accepted it?"

It was as if she could see straight to his soul. "I have no choice. My father never spoke of her. But then, he rarely spoke to me. Perhaps I reminded him too much of her."

"At least you actually knew your real father."

"Not necessarily." The words spilled out of his stupid mouth before he'd had time to reel them back in.

She shifted slightly toward him and laid a palm on his arm. "Are you saying the king wasn't your biological father?"

He saw no reason to conceal his concerns now that he'd taken her into his confidence. "I only know I do not resemble him or my brothers. My hair is lighter and so are my eyes."

"That's not definitive proof, Adan," she said. "Maybe you look like your mother."

"I've seen a few photographs, and I see nothing of me in her. She had almost jet-black hair and extremely dark eyes, like Rafiq."

"If that's the case, then why would you think someone else fathered you?"

"Because my mother was reportedly very unhappy, and I suspect she could have turned to another man for comfort. Rafiq's former wife, Rima, did that very thing due to her own discontent with the marriage."

"Are you certain you're not speculating because of Rafiq's situation?"

He had valid reasons for his suspicions, namely his father's two-decade affair with the governess. Yet he had no intention of skewing Piper's opinion of Elena by revealing the truth yet. "My parents' marriage was arranged, as tradition ordained it. Marriage contracts are basically business arrangements, and in theory advantageous for both families. Unfortunately, when human emotions enter into the mix, the intent behind the agreement becomes muddled."

She frowned. "You mean emotions as in *love?*"

"Yes. The motivating force behind many of the world's ills."

"And the cure for many more."

She didn't sound pleased with his assessment. She had sounded somewhat wistful. "Spoken like a true romantic."

"Spoken like a diehard cynic," she said. "But your cynical days could soon be over now that you have a baby. There is no greater love than that which exists between parent and child, provided the parent is open to that love."

That sounded somewhat like an indictment to his character. "I have already established that bond with my son. But I have never welcomed romantic love for lack of a good example." And for fear of the inability to live up to unreasonable expectations.

She inclined her head and studied him. "Love isn't something you always have to work at, Your Highness. Sometimes it happens when you least expect it."

Piper sounded as if she spoke of her own experiences. "Have you ever been in love?" he asked.

"Not to this point." She glanced away briefly before bringing her attention back to him. "Do arranged marriages still exist in the royal family?"

Happily for him, the answer was no. "That requirement changed after Rafiq inherited the crown. Otherwise he would not have been able to marry a divorced woman. All the better. It was an illogical and worthless tradition, in my opinion."

She offered him a sunny smile that seemed somehow forced. "Well, I guess we really bucked tradition by arranging to have a fake marriage."

At the moment he'd like to have a fake honeymoon, yet he still had reservations. Piper had accommodated the king's wishes by joining in the ruse, and she'd selflessly helped care for his son. He never wanted her to believe he would take advantage of the situation. "Quite frankly, all this talk of family dysfunction is making me weary." He stood and offered his hand. "Would you care to go for a swim?"

"Yes, I most definitely would," she said as she allowed him to help her up. "But are you sure you're up to it? You look tired, and I suspect that has to do with Sam."

"He was awake quite a bit last night and I had the devil of a time getting him back to sleep after the two o'clock feeding. Yet I grew accustomed to little sleep while training for my military duties."

"Why didn't you wake me? I would have taken a shift."

"Because my child is my responsibility, not yours." He immediately regretted the somewhat callous remark and set out to make amends. "I definitely appreciate all that you've done, but I do not want to take advantage of your generosity."

She attempted a smile that failed to reach her blue eyes. "I really don't mind, Adan. What are fake mothers for?"

He could always count on her to use humor to cover her hurt. Hurt that he had caused. "We'll worry about Samuel's care when we return in two days."

Her mouth momentarily dropped open. "Two days? I thought you said this was an afternoon outing."

He endeavored to appear guileless. "Did I?"

She doomed him to hell with a look. "You did."

"My apologies. As it turns out, we have been instructed by the king to remain absent from the palace for two days to avoid the media frenzy. I do think it's best we return tomorrow before sundown. I do not want to be away from Samuel two nights."

"But my grandfather ordered me to see that the engineers finalize the—"

"Bid, and that has been handled by Rafiq. He has accepted, and the contract will be couriered to your grandfather tomorrow. He has also arranged for the engineers to be transported to the States in the morning."

She threaded her lip between her teeth as she took several moments before speaking. "Then I guess everything has been handled."

"Yes, which frees you to relax and see to your own pleasure. Nonetheless, if you insist on returning early, we shall."

This time her smile arrived fully formed. "Where should I change to get this two-day party started?"

He caught her hands and brushed a kiss across her knuckles. "Never change, Piper McAdams. I like you exactly the way you are."

She wrested away, much to his disappointment. "I meant 'change' as in clothes. I need to put on my swimsuit."

He preferred she'd go without any clothes. "You may use the bath downstairs. You'll find it between my study and the guest room, immediately past the kitchen. Or if you prefer, use the one upstairs adjacent to my bedroom. It's much larger."

"Where are you going to change?"

"I hadn't planned on wearing anything at all." He couldn't contain his laughter when he noticed her shocked expression. "I'm not serious, so do not look so concerned. My swim trunks are upstairs."

She began backing toward the entry. "I'll use the downstairs bath while you go upstairs. And I'd better not find you naked in that pool when I come back."

The word *naked* put specific parts of his anatomy on high alert. "At one time that might have been the case, but I have turned over a new leaf."

She paused at the doors and eyed him suspiciously. "A leaf from the player tree?"

He supposed he deserved that. "Believe what you will, but there have not been that many women in my life. None since I ended my relationship with Talia."

"Ah, yes. The celibacy clause. How's that working out for you?"

Not very well at the moment. Not when he knew in a matter of moments he would see her with very little covering her body. Or so he hoped. "I will let you know by day's end."

As soon as she returned to the pool, Piper found Adan staring out over the horizon. She couldn't see his face or eyes, but she sensed his mind was on something else—or someone else, namely his child. Her mind immediately sank into the gutter when she shamelessly studied all the details from his bare, well-defined back to his impressive butt concealed by a pair of navy swim trunks.

She approached him slowly, overwhelmed by the urge to run her hands over the patently male terrain. Instead, she secured the towel knotted between her breasts. "I'm fairly sure that mountain won't move no matter how long you stare at it."

He turned to her, his expression surprisingly somber. "If only I had that power."

Once she moved past the initial shock of seeing his gorgeous bare chest, she found her voice. "Are you worried about Sam?"

"I'm worried that my position will prevent me from being a good father to him. I'm also concerned that perhaps I would be wrong to ask Talia to give up all claims on him."

"No offense, Adan, but I don't see Talia as the motherly type."

"Perhaps so, but isn't any mother better than no mother at all?"

"Not really," she said without thought. "My so-called mother never cared about her daughters. Her own needs took precedence over ours. Luckily for us, my grandmother willingly stepped in and gave us all the love we could ask for, and more. Otherwise I don't know how we would have turned out."

He brushed his knuckles over her cheek. "You have turned out very well. And now if you would kindly remove that towel, we'll spend the afternoon basking in the Bajul sun."

That would be the logical next step—revealing her black bikini that left little to the imagination. A step that required some advance preparation. "Before I do that, you need to know I'm not tall and skinny like Talia. I'm short and I haven't been blessed with a lean build and—"

He flipped the knot with one smooth move and the towel immediately fell to the ground. Then he gave her a lingering once-over before raising his gaze back to her eyes. "You have been blessed with a beautiful body, Piper. You have the curves this man desires."

He desired her curves? Incredible. "Your physique is the thing fantasies are made of. But the question is, how well do you swim? I have to warn you, I'm pretty darned good at it."

And without giving her any warning, he strode to the far end of the pool and executed a perfect dive. He emerged a few moments later, slicked back his hair and smiled. "Now it's your turn to prove your expertise."

If only she could stop gaping at his dimples and get her feet to move. Finally she willed herself to follow his lead by moving to the same spot he had and doing a little diving of her own. After her eyes adjusted, she sought Adan out where he now stood in the shallow end. She remained underwater until she swam immediately in front of him and came up for air. "How's that?"

"Perfect," he said as he put his arms around her. "As are you."

She laughed even though she could barely concentrate while being up close and personal. "Not hardly, Your Majesty. I can be stubborn and I do have a little bit of a temper at times. I'm also a picky eater and I speed when I drive—"

He cut off her laundry list of faults with a kiss. A kiss so hot it rivaled the sun beating down on her shoulders. A down-and-dirty, tongue-dueling kiss that had Piper heating up in unseen places on her person. When he streamed his palms along her rib cage and grazed the side of her breast, she thought she might melt. When he returned his hands to her shoulders, she thought she might groan in protest.

He studied her eyes with an intensity that stole what was left of her breath. "Before this continues, I need to say something."

She needed him to get on with it. "I'm listening."

"I want to make love to you, more than anything I have wished for in some time. But you are under no obligation to honor that request."

Was he kidding? "If I remember correctly, I went to your hotel room in Chicago with that one goal in mind. Of course, where I wanted to end my celibacy, you were determined to hang on to yours."

"Not anymore," he said. "Not since the day I met you, actually. You are different from any woman I have ever known."

"Is that a good thing?"

"A very good thing."

"Then let's put an end to doing without right here and now."

He gave her an unmistakable bad-boy grin. "Take off your suit."

"You go first," she said, suddenly feeling self-conscious.

"All right." He quickly removed the trunks and tossed them aside, where they hit the cement deck with a splat. "Your turn."

After drawing in a deep breath, she reached back and released the clasp, then untied the bow at her neck. Once she had that accomplished, she threw the top behind her, her bare breasts no longer concealed by the water. "Better?"

"Yes, but you're not finished yet."

Time to go for broke. Piper shimmied her bottoms down her legs and kicked them away. Right then she didn't care if they were carried away by the pool pump's current and ended up in another country. "Are you satisfied now?"

"Not quite, but I will be," he said as he pulled her close, took her hand and guided it down his belly and beyond.

When Adan pressed her palm against his erection, Piper blew out a staggered breath. "I do believe I've located an impressive sea creature down below."

"Actually, it's an eel."

"Electric?"

"Highly charged." He brought her hand back to his chest. "But should you investigate further, I fear I will not be able to make it to the bed."

She stood on tiptoe and kissed the cute cleft in his chin. "What's wrong with a little water play?"

"If you're referring to water foreplay, then I am all for that." He wrapped one arm around her waist, then lowered his mouth to her breast while slipping his hand between her thighs simultaneously.

Piper gripped his shoulders and grounded herself against the heady sensations. She felt as if her legs might liquefy with every pass of his tongue over her nipple, every stroke of his fingertip in a place that needed his attention the most.

As badly as she wanted the sensations to go on forever, the climax came in record time. She inadvertently dug her nails into his flesh and unsuccessfully stopped the odd sound bubbling up from her throat.

Once the waves subsided, Piper closed her eyes and sighed. "I'm so sorry that happened so fast," she murmured without looking at him.

He tipped her chin up with a fingertip. "You have no

need to apologize. It has been a while for you, by your own admission."

"Try never."

As she predicted, he was obviously stunned by the truth. "You've never had an orgasm?"

She managed a shrug. "Not with anyone else in the room."

"You clearly have encountered nothing but fools."

Fool, singular. "I've only been intimately involved with one man, and he basically treated me like a fast-food drive-through. In and out as quickly as possible."

Adan released a low, grainy laugh. "I am glad to know you find some humor in the situation. I personally find it appalling when a man has no concern for his lover's pleasure."

She draped her arms around his neck and wriggled her hips. "That goes both ways, and I do believe you are greatly in need of some pleasure. Why bother with a bed when we have a perfectly good pool deck and a comfy-looking chaise at our disposal?"

He kissed her lightly. "True, but we have no condoms."

"I see where that would be a problem."

"A very serious problem. I have already received one unexpected surprise with my son. I do not intend to have another."

Piper wasn't certain if he meant another surprise pregnancy or simply another child, period. Or he could mean he didn't care to have a baby with her. But she refused to let haywire emotions ruin this little temporary piece of paradise, even if it was based on pretense. "Then I suggest you take me to bed, Your Machoness."

No sooner than the words left her mouth, Adan swept

her up into his arms and carried her into the house. She expected him to make use of the downstairs bedroom, but instead he started up the stairs with ease, as if she weighed no more than a feather. Far from the truth. Yet he had a knack for making her feel beautiful. She figured he'd probably earned pro status in the flattery department years ago.

Piper barely had time to look around before Adan deposited her in the middle of the bed covered in a light-weight beige spread. She did have time to assess all his finer details while he opened the nightstand drawer and retrieved a condom. He was evidently very proud to see her, and she was extremely happy to be there. But when he caught her watching, she grabbed the pillow from beneath her head and placed it over her fiery face.

She felt the mattress bend beside her right before he yanked the pillow away. "You're not growing shy on me, are you?" he asked.

No, but she was certainly growing hotter by the second. "I'm just feeling a bit exposed."

He smiled as he skimmed his palm down her belly and back up again. "And I am greatly enjoying the exposure." Then his expression turned oddly serious. "If you have any reservations whatsoever—"

She pressed a fingertip against his lips. "I want this, Adan. I have for a while now."

"Then say no more."

He stretched out and shifted atop her body, then eased inside her. She couldn't speak if she tried. His weight, his powerful movement, captured all her attention. The play of his muscles beneath her palms, the sound of his voice at her ear describing what he felt at that moment, sent her senses spiraling. His broken breaths, the way he tensed signaled he was barely maintaining control. When she lifted her hips to meet his thrust, he groaned and picked up the pace. Only a matter of time before he couldn't hold out, she realized. And then he shuddered with the force of his climax before collapsing against her breasts, where she could feel his heart beating rapidly.

Piper wanted to remain this way indefinitely—with a sexy, skilled man in her arms and a sense of pride that she'd taken him to the limit. She felt unusually brave, and incredibly empowered. Never before had it been this way with Keiler Farnsworth. And the fact that the jerk's name jumped into her brain made her as mad as a hornet. He couldn't hold a candle to Adan Mehdi. She suspected she'd be hard-pressed to find any man who would.

After a few blissful moments ticked off, Adan lifted his head from her shoulder and grinned. "I hope you don't judge me on the expediency of the act."

She tapped her chin and pretended to think. "I'll have to take a point off for that."

He frowned. "You are keeping score?"

"I wasn't until you mentioned it. However, I'm giving you back that point because you are just so darn cute. So no need to despair, because you've earned a perfect ten."

He rolled over onto his back, taking his weight away and leaving Piper feeling strangely bereft. "I will do much better next time," he said in a grainy voice.

Next time couldn't come soon enough for her.

Piper McAdams proved to be more enthusiastic than any woman before her. Adan had recognized that during their second heated round of lovemaking at midnight. And again a few hours ago, immediately before dawn, when she'd awakened him with a kiss before urging him to join her in the shower. They'd spent a good deal of time there bathing each other until he took her up against the tiled wall. Still he could not seem to get enough of her.

Making love to her a fourth time in twenty-four hours seemed highly improbable. He should be completely sated. Totally exhausted. Utterly spent.

"Smells like something good is cooking in the kitchen."

At the sound of her sensual morning voice, Adan glanced over one shoulder to find Piper standing in the opening, wearing his robe. The improbable became possible when his body reacted with a surprisingly spontaneous erection.

"I'm heating up the *ataif* that Ghania prepared." And attempting to hide his sins by paying more attention to the stove than his guest.

"What is *ataif*?" she asked.

Recipe recitation should aid in calming his baser urges. When goats sprouted wings. "*Ataif* is a Middle Eastern pancake dipped in honey and cinnamon and covered in walnuts. It is served with a heavy cream known as *kaymak*."

"Thank you for such a thorough description, Chef Sheikh. Now, who is Ghania?"

He was somewhat surprised she hadn't asked that question first. "Ghania is Qareeb's wife. They're the caretakers. She was kind enough to bring the food by a few moments ago."

"How nice of her."

He afforded her another fast glance before returning to his task. "I received news about my son. According to Maysa, he only awoke one time."

"You have cell towers all the way out here?"

"No. The message arrived by carrier pigeon."

"Very amusing," she said before he felt something hit the back of his head.

He looked down to see a wadded paper napkin at his feet. "No need for violence. If you care to communicate with someone, you may use the phone in my study. It's a direct line to the palace that I had installed in the event a military crisis arises."

"That's good to know, and I'd also like to know why you refuse to look at me. I know my hair's still damp and I don't have on a scrap of makeup, but it can't be all that bad. Or maybe it could."

If she only knew how badly he wanted her, with or without the feminine frills, she would not sound so unsure of herself. "For your information, you are a natural beauty, and I am trying to retain some dignity since it seems I am unable to cool my engine in your presence."

"Still revving to go, are you?"

Piper's amused tone sent him around to face her. And if matters weren't bad enough, she was seated on the high-back bar stool facing him, her shapely thighs completely uncovered due to the split in the white cloth. "Are you naked beneath the robe?"

She leaned back against the stainless steel island, using her elbows for support. "Yes, I am. I forgot to bring panties into the bath before I showered."

He was seconds away from forgetting himself and the food preparation. "Perhaps you should dress before we dine."

She crossed one leg over the other and loosened the sash enough to create a gap at her breasts, giving him a glimpse of one pale pink nipple. "Perhaps we should forgo breakfast for the time being."

That was all it took to commit a culinary cardinal sin by leaving the pan on the burner. But if the whole bloody kitchen went up in flames, it could not rival the heat he experienced at that moment.

Without giving her fair warning, Adan crossed the small space between them and kissed her with a passion that seemed to know no bounds. He untied the robe, opened it completely, pushed it down her shoulders and then left her mouth to kiss her neck. He traveled down her bare torso, delivering more openmouthed kisses, pausing briefly to pay homage to her breasts before continuing down her abdomen. What he planned next could prompt her to shove him away, but he was willing to take a chance to reap the reward—driving her to the brink of sexual insanity. A small price to pay for ultimate pleasure, as she would soon see, if she allowed it.

When Adan parted her knees, he felt her tense and noted apprehension in her eyes. "Trust me, *mon ange,*" he whispered.

She smiled weakly. "Considering I'm half-naked on a bar stool, that would indicate I'm no angel, Adan. But I do trust you. So hurry."

Permission granted, all systems go. He began by lowering to his knees and kissing the insides of her thighs until he felt her tremble. As he worked his way toward his intended target, she shifted restlessly and then lifted her hips toward his mouth in undeniable encouragement. He used gentle persuasion to coax her climax with soft strokes of his tongue, the steady pull of his lips. As she threaded her fingers through his hair and held on firmly, he sensed he would soon achieve his goal. He wasn't the least bit wrong. She released a low moan as the orgasm took over, yet he refused to let up until he was certain she'd experienced every last wave.

Only after he felt her relax did his own desires demand to be met, and so did the need to make haste. He quickly came to his feet, grabbed the condom she'd discarded on the island and ripped open the plastic with his teeth.

Adan had the condom in place in a matter of moments and then seated himself deep inside her. He tried to temper his thrusts, but when Piper wrapped her legs around his waist, restraint left the bungalow. He couldn't readily recall feeling so driven to please a woman. He could not remember the last time he had felt this good. His thoughts disappeared when his own climax came with the force of a missile and seemed to continue for an extraordinary amount of time.

Little by little, logic began to return, including the fact he'd probably turned the cakes into cinders. He lifted his head and sought Piper's gaze. "I fear I have failed in my chef duties."

She reached up and stroked his unshaven jaw. "But you didn't fail me in your lovemaking duties, and that's much more important than breakfast."

For the first time in his life, he'd needed to hear that declaration from a lover. He'd never lacked in confidence or consideration of his partners' needs, yet he had kept his emotions at arm's length with every woman—until now.

But as much as he wanted to please this beautiful woman in his arms, as much as he would like to give more of himself to her, he wasn't certain he could. And if his relationship history repeated itself, he would probably fail her, too.

Seven

After they arrived back at the airbase and boarded the blasted motorcycle again, Piper feared turning prematurely gray thanks to Adan's daredevil driving. Fortunately that wasn't the case, she realized when they entered the palace foyer and she sneaked a peek in the gold-framed mirror. Granted, her hair was a tangled mess, but she couldn't wait a minute longer to see baby Sam.

Adan obviously felt the same, evidenced by his decision to forgo the elevator and take the stairs instead. She practically had to sprint to catch up with him as Abdul, who insisted on carrying her bag, trailed behind them.

Once they reached the third floor, both she and the houseman were winded, while Adan continued toward the nursery as if he possessed all the energy in the world. He actually did, something she'd learned over the past forty-eight hours in his bed. In his shower. In his kitchen and the pool.

Before Adan could open the nursery door, a striking woman with waist-length brunette hair walked out, clearly startled by the sheikh's sudden appearance. "You took years off my life, brother-in-law."

"My apologies, Maysa," he replied, confirming she was the reining queen. "I'm anxious to see about my son."

Maysa closed the door behind her before facing Adan. "I have already put him down for the night and I advise you wait until he wakes. You seem as though you could use some rest." She topped off the comment with a smile aimed at Piper.

Taking that as her cue, she stepped forward, uncertain whether to curtsy or offer her hand. She opted to let the queen make the first move. "I'm Piper McAdams, and it's a pleasure to finally meet you, Your Highness."

"Welcome to the family," she said, then drew Piper into a surprising embrace. "And please call me Maysa."

Piper experienced a fraud alert. "Actually, I'm not really—"

"Accustomed to it yet," Adan interjected. "Given time she will take to the royal treatment as an electric eel takes to water."

Leave it to the prince to joke at a time like this. "I'm not in the market to be treated royally, but I have enjoyed my time in the palace so far."

"I am glad," Maysa said. "Now, if you will both excuse me, I am starving."

Adan checked his watch. "Isn't dinner later than usual?"

Maysa shrugged. "No, but Rafiq is waiting for me in our quarters."

He winked at Piper before regarding Maysa again. "Oh, you're referring to a different kind of appetite. Do not let us keep you from our king."

"You could not if you tried."

Following a slight wave and a smile, Maysa strode down the hallway and disappeared around the corner, leaving Piper alone with the shifty, oversexed sheikh. And she liked him that way. A lot.

He caught her hand and tugged her against him. "Have I told you how much I enjoyed our time together?"

"At least ten times, but I'll never grow tired of hearing it. I'm just sad it's over."

"It doesn't have to be, Piper. You can stay with me in my suite."

She could be entering dangerous emotional territory. "Maybe it should be, Adan. I'll be leaving in a few weeks."

"I know," he said, sounding somewhat disappointed. "All the more reason to spend as much time together before you depart. I am an advocate of taking advantage of pleasure at every opportunity."

How easy it would be to say yes. "I don't know if that's a good idea."

"Since we are to give the impression we are married, what better way than to share the same quarters?"

A false impression of holy matrimony. "We could do that without sleeping in the same bed."

He rimmed the shell of her ear with the tip of his tongue. "I don't recall mentioning sleep."

And she wouldn't get much if she agreed, for several reasons. "You have to consider Sam's needs over ours."

He pulled back and frowned. "Exactly as I intend to do, but he doesn't require all our time during the night."

"He requires quite a bit."

Framing her face in his palms, Adan looked as if his world revolved around her decision. "Stay with me, Piper. Stay until you must leave."

Spending time with this gorgeous Arabian prince, quality time, would be a fantasy come to life. Yet it could never be the real stuff fairy tales were made of. If she took wisdom into account, she'd say no. If she was willing to risk a broken heart, she'd say yes. And she suddenly realized this risk would be well worth undertaking now, even if it meant crying about it later.

"All right, Adan. I'll stay."

In the silence of his private quarters, the room illuminated by the soft glow of a single table lamp, Adan had never experienced such a strong sense of peace. He had the woman curled up next to him to thank for that. Granted, he still wanted Piper in every way imaginable—he'd proved that at his mountain retreat—yet he greatly appreciated the moments they'd spent in comfortable silence after retiring to his quarters.

That lack of conversation would soon end once he told her what he'd learned from his brother upon their arrival a few hours ago. "I have to go to the base tomorrow to oversee training exercises. It will require me to stay in the barracks overnight."

For a moment he'd thought she'd fallen asleep, until she shifted and rested her cheek above his heart. "Gee, thanks. You invite me to reside in your room and then promptly leave me for a whole night."

The teasing quality to her voice gave Adan some semblance of relief. "If I had to choose between sleeping in the barracks with twenty snoring men and sleeping with you, I would choose you every time. Unless you begin snoring—then I could possibly reconsider."

She lightly elbowed him in the rib cage. "If I did happen to snore, which I don't, you'd have no right to criticize me. I thought a freight train had come through the bedroom last night."

"Are you bloody serious?"

"I'm kidding, Adan," she said as she traced a path along his arm with a fingertip. "Your snore actually sounds more like a purr."

That did not please him in the least. "I prefer a freight train to a common house cat."

"Don't worry, Prince Mehdi. Snore or no snore, you're still as macho and sexy as ever."

He pressed a kiss against the corner of her smiling, sensual mouth. "You are now forgiven for the affront to my manhood."

She yawned and briefly stretched her arms over her head. "Have you ever been in live combat before?"

The query took him aback. "Yes, I have."

"Was it dangerous?"

He smiled at the zeal in her voice. "Does that prospect appeal to your daring side?"

"I'm not sure I actually have much of a daring side. I asked because we're presumed to be husband and wife, so I believe it might be prudent for me to learn all I can about you, in case someone asks."

That sounded logical, but not all his military experiences had been favorable. "I've been involved in a skirmish or two while protecting our no-fly zone."

"Bad skirmishes?"

This was the part he didn't speak of often, yet again he felt the need to bare his soul to her. "One turned out to be extremely bad."

"What happened?"

"I killed a man."

He feared the revelation had rendered her speechless, until she said, "I'm assuming it was justified."

"That is a correct assumption. If I hadn't shot down his plane, he would have dropped a bomb over the village."

"How horrible. Was he a citizen of Bajul?"

"No. He was a known insurgent from another country. Because the files are classified, I am not at liberty to say which country."

She lifted her head and kissed his neck before settling back against him. "You don't have to say anything else if you don't want to."

Oh, but he did, though he wasn't certain why. "It happened four years ago," he continued. "That morning I received intelligence about the threat, and I decided I would enter the fray. Later I found out my father was livid, but only because if I perished, he would be without a commander."

"He told you that?" Her tone indicated her disbelief.

"Rafiq informed me, but it doesn't really matter now. I assisted in thwarting an attack that could have led to war for the first time in Bajul's history, and that is what matters. But I never realized…"

"Realized what, Adan?"

He doubted she would let up unless he provided all

the details. "I never knew how affected I would be by sending a man to his death."

"I can imagine how hard on you that must have been."

"Oddly, I had no real reaction to the incident until the following day while briefing our governing council. Midway through the report, I felt as if I couldn't draw a breath. I excused myself and walked outside to regain some composure. That night I had horrible dreams, and they continued for several months."

"I'm so sorry," she said sincerely. "For what it's worth, I think you're a very brave and honorable man. Sam is very lucky to have you as his father."

He'd longed to hear her acknowledge his honor, but he didn't deserve that praise in this situation. "There is no honor in taking another life. And now that I have a son, I will stress that very thing to him."

"That attitude is exactly what makes you honorable," she said. "You were bothered by an evil man's demise to the point of having nightmares. That means you have compassion and a conscience."

If that were the case, he wouldn't have asked her to remain in his quarters for the duration of their time together. Yet he'd not considered anything other than his own needs. And he did need her—in ways he could not have predicted. Still, he couldn't get too close to her or build her expectations beyond what he could provide aside from being her lover. He wasn't suited for a permanent relationship, as his family had told him time and again. "We should try to sleep now. I suspect Samuel will be summoning me in less than two hours."

She fitted her body closer to his side. "I'll be glad to take care of Sam tonight while you get your rest."

"Again, that's not necessary."

"Maybe not, but I really want to do it, not only for you, but for me. We barely caught a glimpse of him tonight. Besides, I'll only have him a little longer, while you'll have him the rest of your life."

Piper's words filled Adan with unexpected regret. Regret that, in a matter of weeks, he would be forced to say goodbye to an incredible woman. In the meantime, he would make the most of their remaining hours together and grant her whatever her heart desired, not only as the provisional mother to his son, but as his temporary lover.

He rolled to face Piper, leaving nothing between them but bare flesh. "Since you have presented such a convincing argument, we will see to Samuel together. Before this, could I convince you to spend the next few hours in some interesting ways?"

She laughed softly. "I thought we were going to sleep."

Bent on persuasion, he skimmed his palm along her curves and paused at the bend of her waist. "We could do that if you'd like."

She draped her arm over his hip. "Sleeping is definitely overrated, so I'm willing to go wherever you lead me."

And she was leading him to a place he'd never been before—close to crashing and burning with no safe place to land. Tonight, he wouldn't analyze the unfamiliar feelings. Tonight, she was all his, and he would treat her as if she always would be.

What an incredible night.

A week ago, Piper would never have believed she

could find a lover as unselfish as Adan. She also couldn't believe her inhibitions had all but disappeared when they made love.

As she supported her cheek with her palm and studied him in the dim light streaming through a break in the heavy gold curtains, she wanted him desperately—even if she was a bit miffed he'd failed to wake her to help care for Sam. Apparently she'd been so relaxed in the postcoitus afterglow, she hadn't heard the baby's cries through the bedside monitor. Some mother she would make.

When Adan stirred, she turned her complete focus on him as he lay sleeping on his back, one arm resting above his head on the navy satin-covered pillow, the other draped loosely across his abdomen. She loved the dark shading of whiskers surrounding his gorgeous mouth, envied the way his long dark lashes fanned beneath his eyes and admired the intricate details of his hand as he slid his palm from his sternum down to beneath the sheet and back up again. The reflexive gesture was so masculine, so sexy, she fought the urge to rip back the covers and climb on board the pleasure express.

Then he opened his eyes and blinked twice before he presented a smile as slow as the sun rising above the mountains. "Good morning, princess."

Didn't she wish. "Good morning. Did you sleep well?"

"Always with you in my bed. How did you sleep?"

"Too soundly. I didn't even hear Sam last night, and evidently you either didn't wake me to help, or couldn't."

He frowned. "I didn't hear him, either."

Simultaneous panic set in, sending them both from the bed and grabbing robes as they hurried out of the bedroom. They practically sprinted toward the nursery and tore through the door, only to find an empty crib.

Piper's hand immediately went to her mouth to cover the gasp. "Someone took him."

"That is impossible," Adan said, a hint of fear calling out from his gold-brown eyes. "The palace is a virtual fortress. If someone kidnapped him, it would have to be an inside job. And if that is the case, I will kill them with my bare hands."

"No need for that, *cara*."

They both spun around to discover Elena sitting in the rocker in the far corner of the lengthy room, the baby cradled in her arms, her expression tinged with disapproval.

Weak with relief, Piper hung back and immediately launched into explanation overdrive. "We never heard him last night. We were both very tired and—"

"The bloody monitor must not be working," Adan added. "Is he all right?"

Elena continued to calmly rock Sam in a steady rhythm. "He is quite fine. And judging from the weight of his diaper when I changed him, I would guess he simply slept all night."

Adan narrowed his eyes and glared at her. "You should have said something the moment we walked into the room."

"You should learn to be more observant of your surroundings when it comes to your son, Adan," she replied. "A hard lesson learned, but one that needed to be taught. When he is toddling, you must know where he is at all times."

Piper, in theory, didn't disagree with the governess's assertions, but she did question her tactics. "We were both expecting to find him in the crib, and needless to say we were shocked when we didn't."

Adan clasped his hands behind his neck and began to pace. "I've been in treacherous military situations less harrowing than this."

Elena pushed out of the chair and approached him. "Settle down, Adan, and hold your baby."

He looked as though he might be afraid to touch him. "I have to prepare for my duties today, but I will return to check on him before I depart for the base."

And with that, he rushed away, leaving Piper alone with the former nanny.

"Well, I suppose I should put this little one to bed for a nap," Elena said, breaking the awkward silence.

Piper approached her and held out her arms. "May I?"

"Of course."

After Elena handed her Sam, Piper kissed his cheek before carefully lowering him to the crib. She continued to study Sam's sweet face slack with sleep, his tiny lips forming a rosebud. He'd grown so much in only a matter of days, and in only a few weeks, she would say goodbye to him—and his father—for good. "He's such a beautiful little boy."

The woman came to her side and rested her slender hands on the top of the railing. "Yes, he is, as his father was at that age."

She saw the chance to learn more about Adan from one of the biggest influences in his life and took it. "Was Adan a good baby?"

"Yes. He was very little trouble, until he turned two,

and then he became quite the terror. He climbed every-thing available to him, and I didn't dare turn my back for more than a second or he would have dismantled something. I would try to scold him over his bad be-havior, and then he would give me that charming smile, and all was forgiven."

Piper could absolutely relate to that. "He was lucky to have you after losing his mother."

Some unnamed emotion passed over Elena's care-worn face. "I was fortunate to have the opportunity to raise him. All the brothers, for that matter."

Time to broach the subject of the paternal presence. "Was the king involved in his upbringing?"

Elena turned and crossed the room to reclaim the rocker, looking as if all the energy had left her. "He did the best that he could under the circumstance. Losing his wife proved to be devastating to him, yet he had no choice but to postpone his grief in order to serve his country."

Piper took the light blue club chair next to Elena. "Adan has intimated the king was a strict disciplinar-ian."

"He could be," she said. "He wanted his sons to be strong, independent men, despite their wealth and their station. Some might say he was too strict at times."

"Would you say that?"

"Perhaps, but it was not my place to interfere."

"I would think you had every right to state your opin-ion in light of your relationship."

Elena stiffened and appeared quite stunned by the statement. "Has Adan spoken to you about myself and the king?"

Piper smelled a scandal brewing. "Not at all. I only

meant that since you were in charge of the children, you should have had some say in how they were treated."

Elena relaxed somewhat, settled back against the rocker and set it in motion. "The king was stern, but fair."

"I'm not sure how fair it was for Adan when he shipped him off to boarding school at such a young age." And she'd probably just overstepped her bounds by at least a mile.

"He did so to protect him."

The defensiveness in her tone did not deter Piper. "Protect him from what?"

Elena tightened her grip on the chair's arms. "I have already said too much."

Not by a long shot, as far as she was concerned. "Look, I don't know what you know, and frankly I don't have to know it. But Adan deserves the truth."

"It would be too painful for him, and would serve no purpose at this point in time."

She wasn't getting through to the woman, which meant she would have to play the guilt card. "Have you ever asked Adan if he would prefer to be kept in the dark? I personally think he wouldn't."

"And you, Ms. McAdams, have not known him all that long."

Touché. "True, but we have spoken at length about his father. Even though he's reluctant to admit it, Adan has a lot of emotional scars, thanks to the king's careless disregard for his youngest son's needs."

She saw the first real hint of anger in Elena's topaz eyes. "Aahil…the king loved Adan. He gave him the very best of everything money could buy, and the opportunity to do what he loved the most. Fly jets."

A perfect lead-in to confront the crux of the matter, yet asking hard questions could be to her detriment. But if Adan could finally put his concerns to rest, it would be worth the risk. "I personally believe he failed to give Adan the one thing he needed most, and that would be a father who paid more attention to him, instead of shipping him far from his home. For that reason, Adan honestly believes the king isn't his biological father."

Elena glanced away, a very telling sign she could be skirting facts. "That is a wrongful assumption."

Piper wasn't ready to give up just yet. "Are you being absolutely honest with me, Elena? And before you speak, keep in mind Adan deserves to know so he could put that part of his past to rest."

"I swear on my papa's grave that the king was very much Adan's biological father."

Even though Elena sounded resolute, Piper couldn't quite help but believe the woman still had something to hide. "Then you need to tell him that, Elena. And you'll have to work hard to convince him, because he's certain something isn't right when it comes to his heritage."

Elena gave her a surprisingly meaningful look. "Do you care for Adan, Ms. McAdams?"

It was her turn to be shocked. "It's Piper, and yes, as one would care for a very good friend." Now she was the one hiding the truth.

"Then I suggest you not worry about things that do not concern you for Adan's sake."

Piper's frustration began to build. "But in some ways they do concern me. I want to see Adan happy and at peace. He can't do that when he knows full well peo- ple are protecting secrets from the past. And no offense, but I believe you're bent on protecting the king and his secrets."

"Are you not protecting Adan and Samuel by masquerading as his wife?"

She had her there. "That's true, but this pretense isn't causing either one of them pain."

"Give it time, Piper," Elena said in a gentler tone. "I can see in Adan's eyes that he cares for you, as well. Perhaps much more than he realizes at this point. But when the fantasy ends and you leave him, reality will be a bitter pill for both of you to swallow. Adan is not the kind of man to commit to one woman, or so he believes."

If Adan did care for her, but he could never be more than her lover, that would possibly shatter her heart completely. But she could still foolishly hope that the man she was dangerously close to loving might change his mind. All the more reason to give him the gift of knowledge, whether he came around or not. "Elena, if you ever cared for Adan at all, I'm imploring you to please consider telling him what you know. Isn't it time to put an end to the mystery and his misery?"

Elena sighed and stared off into space for a few moments before regarding Piper again. "This truth you are seeking will forever change him. He might never accept the mistakes the people in his life have made, even if those mistakes resulted in his very existence."

Finally they were getting somewhere. "Then it's true the queen had an extramarital affair that resulted in Adan's birth."

"No, that is not the case, but you are on the correct path."

Reality suddenly dawned on Piper. "The king had an indiscretion?"

She shook her head. "He had the desire to give the queen what she could not have. A third child. That decision required involving another woman."

"He used a surrogate?" Piper asked, unable to keep the shock from her voice.

"Yes. In a manner of speaking."

"And you know the mother," she said in a simple statement of fact.

Elena knitted her hands together and glanced away. "Very well."

She doubted she would get an answer, but she still had to ask. "Who is she, Elena?"

The woman turned a weary gaze to her and sighed. "I am."

Eight

Piper's brief time in Bajul had been fraught with misunderstanding and mysteries and more than a few surprises. But this bombshell trumped every last one of them. "Who else knows about this?" she asked when she'd finally recovered her voice.

Elena pushed slowly out of the rocker and walked to the window to peer outside. "No one else until now."

All these years, Adan had been living under the assumption that he was another man's child. A supposition that had caused him a great deal of pain, though he had downplayed his burden. But Piper had witnessed it firsthand, and now she wanted nothing more than to finally give him the answers he'd been silently seeking for years. "You have to tell him, Elena."

She turned from the window, a despondent look on

her face. "I have pondered that for many years. I still am not certain it would be wise."

Wise? Surely the former nanny wasn't serious. "Adan deserves to know the truth from the woman who gave him life."

"And he will hate me for withholding that truth for his entire life."

"Why did you withhold it?"

Elena reclaimed the chair and perched on the edge of the cushioned seat. "The king requested that Adan's parentage remain a secret, for both my sake and his."

"You mean for the king's sake, don't you?" She hadn't been able to tamp down the obvious anger in her tone, but she was angry. Livid, in fact.

"For all our sakes," Elena replied. "And for the benefit of the queen, who was already suffering from the decision Aahil made to give her another child."

"But I thought she wanted another baby."

"She did, yet after Adan was born, she could not hold him. In fact, she wanted nothing to do with him. What was meant to give her solace only drove her deeper into depression."

Piper was about to step out on a limb, even knowing it could break the revelations wide-open. "When Adan was conceived, was it through artificial means?"

Elena shook her head. "That process would have included medical staff, and we could not risk involving anyone who might reveal the truth."

"Then Adan was conceived—"

"Through natural means." Once again her gaze drifted away. "And after all was said and done, I am somewhat ashamed to say Aahil and I fell in love during the process, though he continued to be true to the queen until her demise. We remained devoted to each other until his death, and until last year, I kept our relationship a secret."

That meant the king had slept with the governess for the sake of procreation to please his queen, resulting in a decades-long affair. A twisted fairy tale that needed to be untangled. "You said 'until last year.' Does that mean Adan knows you were involved with his father?"

"Yes," she said quietly. "All the boys know. But they do not know I am Adan's true mother."

"It's not too late to rectify the deception, Elena, especially now that Adan has a son. A grandson whom you can acknowledge if you'll just tell Adan the whole story."

Elena's eyes began to mist with unshed tears. "I could not bear to tell him the rest for fear he'll hate me."

Piper leaned forward and clasped Elena's hands. "You're the only mother Adan has ever known, and it's obvious he loves you very much. He might need time to adjust, but I'm sure he'll eventually forgive you."

"It is because of my love for him that I want to protect him from more pain. And you must promise me, Piper, that you will say nothing to him."

The woman drove a hard bargain that could force a wedge between Piper and Adan should he ever learn she'd continued the ruse. "I'll allow you to tell Adan, but—"

"Tell me what?"

Startled by Adan's sudden appearance, Piper quickly shot to her feet. "We were just discussing…actually…"

"We were discussing Samuel's care," Elena said as she gave Piper a cautioning look.

"Am I doing something wrong?" Adan asked, sounding somewhat frustrated.

The lies would surely taste as bitter as brine going down. But it honestly wasn't Piper's place to enlighten him. "You're doing a great job. I basically asked Elena to keep encouraging you when I'm no longer here."

His expression turned somber. "We will discuss that following your departure. At the moment, I need to say goodbye to my son."

Piper remained rooted to her spot as Adan walked to the crib and laid a gentle hand on Sam's forehead. He looked so handsome in his navy flight suit, sunglasses perched atop his head and heavy boots on his feet. He also looked like the consummate father. And when he turned and came to her side, she desperately wanted to blurt out the truth.

Instead, she maintained an overly pleasant demeanor that inaccurately reflected her mood. "I guess we'll see you tomorrow evening, right?"

"Yes, and hopefully not too late." Then he brushed a kiss across her lips, as if this make-believe marriage had somehow become real. She knew better.

"Keep her company, Elena," he said as he kissed her cheek, unaware he was showing affection to his mother. "And do not reveal to her all my bad habits."

Elena reached up and patted his face. "Godspeed, *cara mia.*"

After Adan left the room in a rush, Piper regarded Elena again. "I'll give you my word not to say anything to him, as long as you promise you'll tell him the truth. If you don't, I will."

Elena oddly didn't seem at all upset by the threat. "I will tell him before you depart. And I sincerely hope you will tell him what you have been concealing from him, as well."

That threw Piper for a mental loop. "I'm not hiding anything from Adan."

"Yes, my dear, you are." She started for the door but turned and paused before she exited. "You love him, Piper. Tell him soon."

Long after Elena left the nursery, Piper stood there aimlessly staring at the sleeping baby as she pondered the former governess's words. Did she love Adan? Did she even dare admit it to herself, much less to him?

Yet in her heart of hearts she knew that she did love him, and she loved his son as she would have her own child. Regardless, nothing would come of it unless Adan felt the same way about her. Only time would tell, and time was slowly slipping away.

At half past midnight, Adan arrived at the palace initially exhausted from performing his duties. Yet the moment he entered the corridor leading to the living quarters, his fatigue began to dissipate as he started toward his first stop—the nursery to see his son. After that, he would retire to his bedroom in hopes of finding Piper waiting up for him. He certainly wouldn't blame her if she wasn't, considering the lateness of the hour. And if that happened to be the case, he would use creative kisses in strategic places to wake her.

He found the nursery door open and the room entirely vacant. An empty bottle on the table next to the rocker indicated someone had recently been there to tend to Samuel, and he suspected who that someone might be.

On that thought, he traveled down the hall at a quick

clip, and pulled up short at the partially ajar door when he heard the soft, melodic sounds of a French lullaby.

"Dodo, l'enfant do, l'enfant dormira bien vite. Dodo, l'enfant do. L'enfant dormira bientôt."

The lyrics alone indicated Piper could be having difficulty putting Samuel to sleep, but Adan imagined her sweet voice would eventually do the trick. He stayed in the hallway, immersed in faint memories of Elena singing him to sleep. Sadly he'd never had the pleasure of recalling his own mother doing the same.

He wondered if Samuel would eventually resent him for taking him away from Talia. Provided Talia actually agreed to signing over her rights, and he didn't change his mind about asking her to do that very thing.

The sudden silence thrust the concerns away and sent Adan into the bedroom. He discovered Piper propped up against the headboard, eyes closed, her dark hair fanning out on the stack of white satin pillows beneath her head, and his son, deep in slumber, cradled against her breasts. Had she not been gently patting the baby's back, he might have believed she'd fallen asleep, as well.

He remained in place, recognizing at that moment how greatly he appreciated this woman who had stepped in to care for his child without hesitation. He'd begun to care for her deeply, more than he had any woman. But to expect her to continue in this role much longer would be completely unfair to both her and his child. She had another life in another country, and she would soon return to resume that life.

When Piper opened her eyes and caught his glance, she smiled before holding a finger against her lips to ensure his silence. He waited at the door as she worked her way slowly off the bed and approached him at the door. "I'll be right back," she whispered. "Unless he wakes again."

Unable to resist, he softly kissed the top of Samuel's head, remarkably without disturbing him, then leaned and kissed Piper's cheek, earning him another smile before she left the room.

In order to be waiting in bed for her return, Adan launched into action. He stripped out of his clothes on his way into the bathroom, turned on the water in the shower, then stepped beneath the spray and began to wash. He'd barely finished rinsing when the glass door opened—and one beautiful, naked woman with her hair piled atop her head boldly joined him.

Using his shoulders for support, she stood on tiptoe and brought her lips to his ear. "I missed you."

He framed her face in his palms. "I missed you, too."

All conversation ceased as they explored each other's bodies with eager hands as the water rained down over them. They kissed with shared passion, touched without restraint. Adan purposely kept Piper on the brink of orgasm with light pressure before he quickened the pace. She released a small moan, then raked her nails down his back with the force of her release. He soon discovered she was bent on reciprocating when she nudged him against the shower wall, lowered to her knees and took him into her mouth. He tipped his head back and gritted his teeth as she took him to the breaking point. Refusing to allow that to happen, he clasped her wrists and pulled her to her feet.

"Not here," he grated out, then swept her into his arms, carried her into the bedroom and brought her down on the sheets despite the fact they were soaking wet.

He slowed the tempo then, using his mouth to bring her more pleasure as she had done with him, until his own body demanded he hurry. In a matter of moments, he had the condom in place, and seated himself soundly inside her. She sighed when he held her closer, yet he couldn't seem to get close enough, even when she wrapped her legs around his waist.

All the unfamiliar emotions, the desperate desire, culminated in a climax that rocked him to the core. He had difficulty catching his breath as his heart beat a thunderous tempo against his chest. Piper began to stroke his back in a soothing rhythm, bringing him slowly back into reality. And that reality included an emotion he'd always rejected in the past. An expression he had never uttered to any lover. A word he dared not acknowledge now, for in doing so he would be completely vulnerable to a woman who was bound to leave.

He preferred to remain as he'd always been, immune to romantic love. Yet as Piper whispered soft words of praise, he wondered where he would find the strength to let her go. He would find it. He had no choice.

But not now. Not tonight.

Three weeks gone, one more to go.

As the first morning light filtered in from the part in the heavy gold curtains, Piper couldn't stop thinking about how little time she had left before she went home. And as she lay curled up in the empty bed, hugging a pillow, she also couldn't stop pondering Adan's abrupt change in mood.

For the past several days, he'd begun to spend more time with the baby when he wasn't at the base and a lot less time with her. She felt somewhat guilty for even questioning his paternal role, but she didn't quite understand why he'd started coming to bed in the middle of the night. Nor could she fathom why they hadn't made love in over a week when they hadn't missed a day since their first time together.

She questioned whether Elena had told him her secret, but she felt certain Adan would have told her if that had been the case. Blamed her for meddling, for that matter. Maybe the prince was simply preparing for their parting. Maybe the pretend princess would be wise to do the same. But lately she'd learned to lead with her heart, not her head. Her head told her to accept the certain end to their relationship. Her heart told her not to go down without a fight.

At the moment, her heart made more sense. For that reason, she climbed from beneath the covers to confront the missing sheikh, who she presumed was still in the nursery, tending to his son. After donning her robe, she padded down the hall to confirm her conjecture. And she did when she walked into the nursery and found Adan in the rocker, Sam cradled against his shoulder, both fast asleep.

All her previous concerns disappeared as she took in the precious sight. A scene worthy of being commemorated on canvas. Regrettably she didn't have one readily available, but she did have a sketch pad.

With that in mind, she hurried back to the bedroom she hadn't occupied in weeks, retrieved paper and pencil and then returned to the nursery. She moved closer to achieve a prime vantage point of father and son in the throes of blissful sleep. A souvenir to take with her that would enhance the wonderful memories…unless…

As she sketched the details with second-nature

strokes, a plan began brewing in her mind. A good plan. She quietly backed out the door and returned to Adan's quarters, closed the door, hid the pad in her lingerie drawer beneath her panties and picked up the palace phone. She expected Elena to answer, but instead heard an unfamiliar female voice ask, "May I help you?"

"Yes. This is…" The sheikh's fake spouse? The prince's bed buddy? She couldn't stomach lying again, even to a stranger. "With whom am I speaking?"

"My name is Kira," she said, her pleasant voice not even hinting at a Middle Eastern accent. "And you are the newest princess."

Apparently the woman thought Piper had forgotten her title. Bogus title. "Right. Is there someone available who could run an errand for me?"

"I will be up immediately."

Before she could offer to come downstairs, the line went dead, allowing her only enough time to brush her teeth and hair before she heard the knock.

After tightening the robe's sash, Piper opened the door to find a woman with golden-brown shoulder-length hair and striking cobalt eyes. She wore a navy blazer covering a white blouse and matching knee-length skirt, sensible pumps and a sunny smile. "Good morning, Princess Mehdi."

Piper would like to return the sentiment, but so far the morning hadn't started off well when she'd woken up alone. "Thank you for answering the summons so quickly, Kira, but this errand isn't really that pressing. I'm not even sure it's possible."

Kira straightened her shoulders and slightly lifted

her chin. "This is only my second day as a palace employee, and it is my duty to make this task possible."

Talk about pressure. "Okay, then. Is there a store that sells art supplies in the village?"

Kira seemed to relax from relief. "Thankfully, yes there is."

Things could be looking up after all. "Great. I need a canvas, the largest one available, and a basic set of oil paints today, if at all possible."

"I will gladly see to the purchase myself."

"Wonderful." Piper hooked a thumb over her shoulder. "I'll just grab my credit card and—"

"That is not necessary," Kira said. "The household budget covers all your expenses."

She didn't have the energy or desire to argue. "I truly appreciate that. And out of curiosity, are you from Bajul? I ask because you don't really have an accent."

"I was born and grew up here but I've been living in Montreal for the past few years. My mother was Canadian, and while she was working in Dubai, she traveled to the queen's mountain resort here one weekend, met my papa, fell madly in love and never left."

At least someone's whirlwind affair had turned out well. "That's a wonderful story. Now, if you don't mind, I have one more favor to ask."

"Whatever you wish, Princess Mehdi."

She really wished she would stop calling her that. "Please, call me Piper."

Kira looked just this side of mortified over the suggestion. "That would not be proper. I am a member of the staff and you are a member of the royal family."

Little did the woman know, nothing could be further from the truth. "How old are you, Kira, if you don't mind me asking?"

She looked a little confused by the question. "Twenty-seven."

"And I'll turn twenty-seven in three months. Since we're basically contemporaries, I'd prefer you address me by my given name while we're in private. If we're in a public forum, we'll adhere to all that ridiculous formality since it's expected. And in all honesty, I could use a friend in the palace. A female friend close to my age."

That brought the return of Kira's grin. "I suppose we could do that. A woman can never have an overabundance of friends."

Piper returned her smile. "Great. Now about that other favor." She gestured Kira inside the suite and closed the door. "Please don't say anything to anyone about the art supplies. I want to surprise Adan."

She raised her hand as if taking an oath. "I promise I will not say a word to the prince, even if it means residing in the dungeon while being subjected to torture."

"There's a dungeon?"

Kira chuckled. "Not that I have seen. And I apologize. At times I let my questionable sense of humor overtake my sound judgment."

"Well, Kira, since I'm prone to do the same, I believe that will make us fast friends. We can meet weekly and exchange smart remarks to enable us to maintain a certain amount of decorum."

They both shared in a laugh then, but all humor ceased when Adan came through the door without warning. He gave Piper a confused look before his gaze settled on Kira—and he grinned. "Are my eyes deceiving me, or has the caretaker's daughter come home?"

"No, Your Highness, your eyes are not deceiving you. I have returned, and I am now working in the palace with the sole intent to serve you."

He frowned. "Serve me grief no doubt, and what is with the 'Your Highness'? If I recall, I was the first boy to kiss you."

"And if I recall, I slugged you before you could."

This time Adan and Kira laughed, before he grabbed her up and spun her around, indicating to Piper this pair knew each other well. Possibly very well. She couldn't quell the bite of jealousy, even though she sensed nothing aside from camaraderie between the two. Or maybe she was just playing the ostrich hiding its head in the desert sand.

After Adan let Kira go, he kept his attention on her. "I thought you were engaged to be married."

"That didn't work out," she replied. "It's a long, sad story that is not worth telling. Luckily Mama and Papa mentioned my return to Elena, and here I am."

Adan finally regarded Piper. "Kira's parents were members of the household staff for many years."

"My father tended the palace grounds," Kira added. "My mother was the head chef at the palace."

Adan pointed at her. "And she was the resident holy terror in her youth."

Kira frowned. "If I were not your subordinate, I would possibly slug you again. But since I am, I will leave you both to your privacy as I have an important task to oversee. Princess Mehdi, it was a pleasure to meet you." She then did an about-face and left, closing the door behind her.

"She certainly left in a hurry," Piper said. "Evidently she had a very bad breakup."

Adan's good spirits seemed to dissolve right before Piper's eyes. "More often than not, relationships run their course and usually come to a less than favorable conclusion."

Piper's hope that he might have feelings for her beyond gratitude evaporated like early-morning fog. "I had no idea you were that cynical, Your Highness."

He disappeared into the closet and returned with khaki cargo pants, a navy T-shirt, socks and a pair of heavy boots. "I am a realist."

She leaned a shoulder against the bedpost as he shrugged out of his robe, finding it difficult to ignore his board-flat abdomen and the slight stream of hair disappearing beneath the waistband of his boxer briefs. "It seems to me both your brothers are happily married."

He tugged the shirt over his head, ruffling his dark hair in the process. "Perhaps, but they are the exception to the rule."

"Your relationship rules?"

He put on his pants one leg at a time and zipped them closed. "I didn't make the rules, Piper. I'm only acknowledging that failed relationships seem to be my forte."

"Are you referring to Talia?"

After rounding the bed, he perched on the mattress's edge to put on his boots. "Yes, among a few other non-intimate relationships, including my father."

Now they were getting somewhere. "You didn't fail him, Adan. He failed you."

"I suppose you're right. Apparently I never accomplished anything to suit him, no matter how hard I tried."

"Even learning to pilot jets wasn't good enough?"

He came to his feet and faced her. "I have no idea since he rarely mentioned my skills, even when he convinced the counsel to appoint me as the armed forces commander."

"Well, at least he had enough faith in you to believe you could handle the responsibility."

"Or he was possibly setting me up to fail. Fortunately I proved him wrong."

She smiled. "Yes, you did, at that. And if it's any consolation, I'm proud of your accomplishments, both military and paternal."

Discomfort called out from his eyes. "You never did say why Kira was here."

Time to lighten the mood. Or die trying. "She was seeking donations for the poor. I told her to take five or so of the watches in your extensive collection since I'm sure they'll go for a hefty price, and you probably wouldn't miss them."

From the sour look on his face, her efforts at levity had fallen flat. "Try again, Piper."

She folded her arms beneath her breasts and sighed. "If you must know, I sent her into the village for a few feminine unmentionables. But I'll be glad to show you the list if you're worried we were somehow plotting against you."

He held up both hands, palms forward. "That will not be necessary. I presently need to prepare for the day."

"Are you going to the base?"

"Not today. Following breakfast, I thought I would

take Samuel for a stroll around the grounds as soon as he wakes from his morning nap."

"Do you mind if I join you?"

"That is entirely up to you."

The lack of enthusiasm in his response told Piper all she needed to know—she wasn't welcome, and that stung like a bumblebee. "I'll let you and Sam have some father-and-son alone time. Besides, I have something I need to do anyway." Namely begin painting a portrait that would serve as a gift for the prince. A parting gift.

"That is your prerogative," he said in a noncommittal tone as he started to the door. "I'll tell the cook to keep your breakfast warm while you dress."

She wasn't hungry for food, but she was definitely starved for answers. "Before you leave, I have something I need to tell you."

Adan paused with his hand on the doorknob and turned to face her. "I'm listening."

She drew in a deep breath and prepared for the possibility of having her heart completely torn in two. "I'm in love with you."

He looked as if she'd slapped him. "What did you say?"

"Don't be obtuse, Adan. I love you. I didn't plan it. I really didn't want it. But it happened in spite of my resistance. My question is, how do you feel about me?"

He lowered his eyes to the floor. "I cannot be the man you need, Piper."

"That's my decision to make, not an answer."

His gaze snapped to hers. "You deserve someone who can give you the emotional support you require."

Meaning he didn't return her feelings. Or maybe he

refused to admit it. Only one way to find out. "What are you afraid of, Adan?"

"I'm not afraid, Piper. As I've said, I'm pragmatic."

"No, you're not," she said. "You're a risk taker, but you're scared to take a chance on us."

"I am only considering your well-being. I do care about you, Piper. Perhaps more than I've cared for any woman in my past. But I'll be damned if I break your heart because I cannot succeed at being faithful to one woman."

The surprising revelations took Piper aback. "Did you cheat on Talia during the six years you were together?"

"No."

"Have you cheated on any woman you've been with?"

"No, but—"

"Then why would you believe you would be unfaithful to me?"

"Because I could be genetically predisposed to adultery, compliments of my mother."

She could no longer allow him to think that his mother had taken a lover who resulted in his birth, in spite of her promise to Elena. Not when their future together could depend on the truth. "Adan, your mother was—"

The sharp rap suspended Piper's confession midsentence and caused Adan to mutter a string of Arabic words as he opened the door.

Piper expected a member of the staff. What she got was Adan's erstwhile lover, her platinum hair slicked back in a low chignon, her lithe body tightly encased in a blue silk jumpsuit, her makeup applied to perfection and her red painted lips curled into a snarl-like smile.

"Surprise, you bleedin' bastard. I'm back!"

Nine

The woman in the catsuit looked ready for a catfight, but Piper wasn't about to bite. "I'll leave you two with your privacy," she said as she targeted the door as her means to escape.

Talia stormed into the room, blocking her escape. "Oh, do stay, chicky. The party is only getting started."

Adan stepped to Piper's side and moved slightly in front of her. "Calm down, Talia. If anyone has cause to be irritated, it should be me. You might have had the courtesy of notifying me of your impending arrival."

"And you might have told me you married—" she pointed a finger at Piper "—this wench."

"Piper is not a wench," Adan stated with a touch of venom in his tone. "And your argument is with me, not her. If you will join me in my study, we will discuss our son."

Talia smirked. "Here seems fine. After all, you've obviously been taking care of the bonking business in the bedroom with her for quite some time, according to the press."

And Piper had only thought they'd covered all their media bases. "You can't believe everything you hear or read, Talia. Adan has done whatever it takes to protect Sam."

The woman nailed her with a seething glare. "Our son is not your concern."

"But he is my concern," Adan said. "And I am prepared to offer you a sizable settlement in exchange for retaining full custody of Samuel."

Talia flipped a hand in dismissal. "Your attorneys have already worked that out with my attorneys."

Adan's expression was a mixture of confusion and anger. "How is that possible when I have not consulted the palace barrister?"

"Maybe you should talk to your brother about that," Talia replied.

"The king knew you were coming?" Piper chimed in, earning a quelling look from Adan.

"Yes, he did," she said. "I had Bridgette call when I arrived back in Paris. Rafiq wouldn't let me speak to you, the duffer, so I hopped on a plane and came here. He practically met me at the door with the papers. I signed them and then I had to evade the houseboy on my way up here."

Piper knew very little British slang, but it didn't take much to interpret Talia's words. "Then I assume you're okay with giving Adan full custody," she said, sticking her nose in where it obviously didn't belong.

Talia screwed up her face in a frown. It wasn't pretty.

"No. I'm giving him to Adan. What would I need with a kid?"

A litany of indictments shot into Piper's brain, threatening to spill out her mouth. Luckily Sam's cry filtered through the monitor at that exact moment, supplying an excuse to bail before she blew up. "I'll take care of him." She brushed past Talia, resisting the urge to rip the expensive designer bag from her shoulder and stomp on it for good measure.

She took a few calming breaths as she quickly made her way to the nursery to see about the baby. The minute she walked into the room, Sam's cries turned into wails, as if he somehow sensed the stressful situation brewing down the hall.

"What's wrong, sweetie?" she said as she picked him up from the crib. "Did you have a bad dream or just need some company?"

His sobs turned to sniffles as she cradled him in her arms, and then she realized he was in dire need of a diaper change. After she saw to that task, she considered instituting Adan's plan to take the baby for a stroll around the grounds. She discarded that idea when she remembered she was still wearing her robe. Nothing like giving tabloid reporters more fuel for gossip should she get caught on camera. Of course, if any of the bottom-feeders had been hanging around in the past hour, which they had been periodically known to do since she'd arrived in Bajul, they would have a field day with Toxic Talia.

Her anger came back full throttle when she considered how the woman had agreed to relinquish her child without a second thought. Couldn't she see what a precious gift she'd been given? Of course she couldn't. She wasn't concerned about anything that didn't promote her personal gain…just like her own mother.

Piper refused to make this decision easy on the selfish supermodel, and with that goal in mind, she strode back down the hall with Sam in tow. She arrived at the open door to the suite in time to hear Talia say, "Now that everything's settled, I'll be on my way."

"You're not going anywhere yet," Piper said through gritted teeth. "Not until you take a good long look at what you're giving away."

Talia spun around and rolled her eyes. "For the last time, this is none of your business, ducky."

Undeterred, Piper walked right up to her and turned the baby around in her arms. "Look at him, Talia, and think about what you're doing. It's still not too late to change your mind."

Adan took a few steps forward. "It's no use, Piper. She's made her choice, and she chooses her career. She wants no part in raising him."

Ignoring Adan, Piper kept her gaze trained on Talia. "This is a life-altering decision. There's no turning back if you walk away now. Is that what you really want?"

A spark of indecision showed in Talia's eyes. "I can't raise him," she said, an almost mournful quality to her voice.

Piper's disdain lessened as she witnessed the woman's defenses began to crumble, one fissure at a time. "Are you absolutely sure?"

"If I were a different person, perhaps I could. But I'm never going to be good at it, and it would be unfair to him if I tried." Then she surprisingly reached out and touched Sam's fisted hand. "So long, little fellow. Be good for your daddy and your new mum."

Talia hurried out the door, but not before Piper caught a glimpse of tears in her eyes. "Maybe I misjudged her," she said as she placed Sam against her shoulder. "Maybe for the first time in her life, she's doing something unselfish."

Adan shoved a hand in his pocket, rubbed his neck with the other and began to pace. "Do you find it odd that all three of us have been betrayed by our mothers?"

In a way, he was right, but not completely. Piper had intended to tell him the truth before Talia's interruption. She now recognized she walked a fine line between breaking a promise and bringing him peace. Perhaps she could avoid crossing that line by handing him only a partial truth. "There are some things you don't know about your mother, and it's high time you do."

He faced her and frowned. "What are you talking about?"

"You need to ask Elena," she said. "She holds the answers, and she's prepared to tell you."

At least that was what she hoped.

A few moments later, Adan found himself standing outside Elena's private office, his mind caught in a maze of confusion. He had no idea what Piper had been talking about, yet he suspected he would soon find out, even if he wasn't certain he wanted to know.

When he rapped on the frame surrounding the open door, Elena looked up from her position behind the desk, obviously startled before surprise melted into a smile. "Come in, *cara*."

He entered, pulled back the chair opposite her and sat. "Am I interrupting anything?"

"Of course not. You are always welcome here."

He stretched out his legs in an attempt to affect a casual demeanor, when in truth his nerves were on edge. "Talia stopped by to sign over custody of Samuel."

"I heard," she said. "And I am very sorry that your son will not have the opportunity to know his mother. On the other hand, since I do know his mother's shortcomings, the decision she made was the best course of action in this case."

"Piper suggested it was an uncharacteristically unselfish act on Talia's part."

"Piper is correct, but then she has wisdom beyond her years."

The moment had arrived to transition into his real reason for being there. "And continuing on with the subject of motherhood, Piper also informed me you had information about my mother that she's convinced I should know."

Unmistakable panic showed in Elena's eyes. "I told her I would tell you in due time."

"Perhaps that time is now."

Elena hesitated for several moments, leading him to believe she might thwart his attempts at garnering information. "I suppose you are right."

"Then proceed," he said as he braced for the possibilities and prepared for the worst.

She picked up a stack of papers and moved them aside before folding her hands atop the desk. "First of all, I must clarify an incorrect assumption you have long held regarding your parents. Your mother always remained true to her husband during their marriage, and they both grew to love each other. Most important, Aahil Mehdi was your biological father, not some unknown man."

He had waited all his life for confirmation or a denial of his theory, yet something didn't quite ring true. "If that is a fact, then why was I the only son not raised and schooled here at the palace? Why was I the only brother sent away during my formative years?"

"To protect you, Adan."

"From what?"

"The chance someone could learn your true parentage, and you would suffer the consequences from being labeled the child of a concubine."

Anger began brewing immediately beneath the surface of his feigned calm. "Then you are saying my father was the adulterer and I am the product of his affair with a servant?"

"No. Your father was a good man, but you were the reminder of his failure to make his queen happy by giving her the baby she was not able to conceive." She sent him a wistful smile. "Yet you were the greatest joy in my life from the moment you came into this world."

Awareness barreled down on him with the force of a hundred wild horses. "*You* gave birth to me?"

"Yes, *cara,* as a favor to the king, and during the process of conception, your father and I fell in love. And as you already know, that love continued until his death, but I assure you we did not act on it until the queen's demise."

Questions continued to bombard his brain. He chose the one that took precedence over all. "Why did you wait to tell me this?"

"I promised your father I would never reveal the truth to anyone, even you."

Once the initial shock subsided, ire took its place.

"He had no right to ask that of you, and you had no right to keep this from me all these years."

"I realize that now," she said. "And had Piper not come to me and then pressed me to reveal the truth to you, I might have carried the secret to my grave."

Adan was torn between gratitude and resentment aimed toward both Elena and Piper. "How long has she known about this secret?"

"For a while."

One more betrayal in a long line of many. "She should have told me immediately."

"Do not blame Piper for not saying anything, Adan. I begged her to allow me to tell you."

"She should not have come to you in the first place."

"She did so because she loves you, Adan. She only wants what is best for you, and she believes with this information you'll find some peace."

Piper's declaration of love intruded into his thoughts, but he pushed it aside. "If that is so, then why would she subject me to this confession knowing it would cause such turmoil?"

"I suspect she recognizes that lies have the capacity to destroy relationships."

And so could the truth. His relationship with Piper had been fraught with lies from the beginning, and he wasn't certain he could trust her now.

Bent on a confrontation, he shoved the chair back and stood. "We will discuss this further after I have had time to digest this information."

Tears filled Elena's eyes. "Please tell me you do not hate me, Adan."

How could he hate the woman who had been the only

mother he had ever known? In reality, his real mother. "I could never hate you, Elena."

"But you might never forgive me," she said, resignation in her tone.

"I will try, and that is all I can promise at this moment," he said before he turned to leave.

"Where are you going, Adan?" Elena called after him.

"To have a serious conversation with my alleged wife."

"What possessed you to interfere in my life?"

Piper put down the art book she'd attempted to read in the common sitting area, moved to the edge of the uncomfortable chair and faced Adan's wrath head-on. "I assume Elena told you everything."

He released a caustic laugh. "You would be correct in that assumption, and you have yet to answer my question."

"Okay. You see it as interference, and I see it as making an effort to find the answers you've always longed for."

"I never sought those answers for a reason."

"And that reason is?"

"I knew nothing good would come of them, and nothing has."

She couldn't believe his attitude or his misdirected anger. "What's not good about finally knowing the identity of your real mother? Believe me, Sunny and I unsuccessfully tried to find our father, but we could only narrow it down to three prospects. One was in prison for insider trading, one was a money-hungry gigolo and the last was married with four children. With that field of prospects, we decided it wasn't worth pursuing. At least you now know you have a wonderful mother."

He ran a fast hand over his jaw. "I am not you, Piper. I had no desire to learn the truth. And now that I do know, I have been shown that even the most trustworthy person is capable of the ultimate betrayal."

She felt as if he'd placed her in that category, along with his biological mother. "Look, Adan, I don't agree with Elena concealing the truth for such a lengthy period of time, but on some level I did understand why she was afraid to reveal it. Seeing your reaction only validated her fears."

He paced back and forth like a caged animal before pausing before her. "How would you wish me to react, Piper? Should I be celebrating the lies I've been told my entire life? Or the fact that you knew the truth and concealed it?"

"Believe me, keeping it from you wasn't easy." A colossal understatement. "But it wasn't my place to tell you, although I would have before I left if Elena hadn't."

He narrowed his eyes into a hard glare. "It wasn't your place to go on a bloody fact-finding mission, either."

No matter how hard she tried to see it from his point of view, his condemnation hurt like the devil. Time to fight fire with fire. "Sometimes it's necessary to set a lie into motion to protect those you love, just like you're protecting Samuel by lying about our marriage."

"You are absolutely correct," he said, taking her by surprise. "And I plan to put an end to that fabrication immediately. Now that Talia has relinquished her rights, you have no cause to remain here any longer. I will make the arrangements for you to fly home as soon as possible."

As she came to her feet, she seriously wanted to cry, maybe even beg, but instead called on fury to give her strength. "So that's it, huh? I've served my purpose and now you're going to toss me out into the street like refuse?"

"I am not tossing you out," he said. "I am giving you back your freedom."

And he was going to hold her emotionally captive for a very long time. But deep down, hadn't she known all along this would happen? And she'd been an unequivocal fool to believe otherwise. "Shame on me for believing I meant more to you than just a quick fix to save your sterling reputation. And shame on you for leading me to believe you were honorable."

She could tell by the harsh look on his face she'd delivered a knockout blow. "I would be less than honorable if I kept you here any longer when we both know that I will never be able to give you what you need."

Battling the threatening tears, Piper snatched up the book and clutched it to her heart. "You're right, Your Highness. I need a man who can let down his guard and take a chance on love, even though I've recently discovered love is a risky business. But just remember, there's a little boy who's going to need all the love you can give him, since, like his father, he's never going to know his mother. Don't fail him because you're too afraid to feel."

Without giving him a chance to respond, Piper stormed down the hall to the make-believe lovers' hideaway, slammed the door behind her and started the process of packing. Only then did she let the tears fall at will and continued to cry until she was all cried out, though she inherently knew she was only temporarily done with the blubbering.

Not long after Piper finished filling the last of the suitcases, a series of knocks signaled a guest had come calling, the last thing she needed. Unless… On the way to answer the summons, she couldn't help hoping Adan had somehow come to his senses and decided to ask for a second chance. That he would appear on the threshold on bended knee with his heart in his hands and a declaration of love flowing from his gorgeous mouth. As if that fairy-tale scenario was going to happen. Most likely she'd find Abdul standing in the hall with his head slightly bowed, a live-to-serve look on his face while he declared his unwavering need to carry her luggage.

She discovered she'd been wrong on both counts when she opened the door to the ever-smiling Kira. "I'm so sorry to bother you, Your—" She sent a quick glance over her shoulder. "…Piper, but the art shop didn't have any canvases available and they only had colored chalk. They did offer to order the supplies for you."

She'd forgotten all about the painting she'd planned to give Adan. "That's okay. I won't be needing those supplies now." Or ever.

Kira appeared sorely disappointed. "But you seemed so excited over surprising your husband."

He's not my husband, she wanted to say, but opted for a partial truth. "I probably shouldn't mention this, but you'll know soon enough. The marriage isn't working out, so I'm returning home this afternoon."

Kira hid a gasp behind her hand. "I am so sorry, Piper. I was so certain seeing you and Adan together today that you were completely in love."

"Love isn't always enough, Kira," she said without thought.

"I know that all too well, Piper."

She sensed her newfound friend did, at that. "Oh, well. Nothing ventured, nothing gained, as they say. And I'm going to miss having the opportunity to get to know you."

"Surely I'll see you when you bring the baby to visit his father."

If only that were the case. Leaving Sam would be equally as difficult as leaving his father behind, never knowing what might have been. "Adan is going to have full custody. I travel a lot with my job and we both think it's important Sam grows up in his homeland with his people."

"But you'll be coming here to see him often, right?"

And now for the final, and most painful, lie. "Of course."

That prompted the return of Kira's smile. "That's wonderful. We can still have those smart-remark sessions when you're here."

"I'd offer to have one now, but I want to give Sam one last bottle before I go."

As Piper stepped into the hall to do that very thing, Kira drew her into a hug. "Goodbye for now, Piper. I wish you the best of luck."

"Same to you," she replied as she started toward the nursery, before she gave in to the temptation to tell Kira the truth.

As much as she wanted to see the cherished baby boy, Piper dreaded telling him goodbye. That didn't prevent her from lifting the sleeping Sam from his crib and holding him for the very last time. He opened his eyes slowly and didn't make a sound, as if he understood the importance of the moment. She walked around the room as one more time she sang the lullaby she'd used to put him to sleep. If only she could be his mother. If only his father had loved her back. If only...

"The car is waiting, Your Highness."

Piper wanted to tell Abdul it would just have to wait, but she saw no use in prolonging the inevitable farewell to the second love of her life. She kissed Sam's forehead, laid him back in the crib and managed a smile. "I love you, sweetie. I know you'll forget me once I'm gone, but I will never forget you."

Or the man who had given him life.

After one last look at Sam, Piper turned to go, only to discover Adan standing in the open door looking somewhat remorseful. "I did not want you to leave before I expressed my gratitude for all that you've done for myself and Samuel."

She truly wanted to tell him what he should do with that gratitude, but she couldn't. She honestly wanted to hate him, and she couldn't do that, either. "You're welcome, Your Highness. It's been quite the adventure."

He attempted a smile that didn't quite reach his eyes. "Yes, it has. And I also want to assure you that I will treat my son as he should be treated. I will make certain he has all that he desires."

Too bad he couldn't promise her the same. "Within reason, I hope. I'd hate to think you'd buy him his first plane on his first birthday."

He favored her with a dimpled grin. The same grin she'd noticed the first time she'd laid eyes on him. "Rest assured I will withhold that gesture until his second birthday."

"Good idea. We wouldn't want him to be too spoiled."

A lengthy span of silence passed as they remained quiet, as if neither knew what to say next. Piper had already said what she'd needed to say when she'd told him she loved him, even if he hadn't done the same. Now all that remained was the final goodbye. "Well, I guess I need to get my things and take to the friendly skies. I'd like to say give me a call if you're ever in need of ending your celibacy, but that wouldn't be wise."

He streaked a palm over the nape of his neck. "I suppose it wouldn't be, at that."

"And just so you know, I don't regret the time we've spent together. I only regret this little fake fairy tale didn't have a happy ending. But that's life. Goodbye, Adan."

When she tried to make a hasty exit, Adan caught her arm and pulled her into an embrace that didn't last nearly long enough. "You are a remarkable woman, Piper McAdams. I wish for you only the brightest future with a deserving man."

She was convinced he could be that man, if only he believed it, which he didn't.

Piper began backing away, determined to leave him with a smile. "I'm going to forgo the whole man-hunting thing for a while, but I've decided I am going to further pursue a career in art."

"I am pleased to hear that," he said sincerely. "Perhaps you can send me some of your work in the future. I will pay top price."

How badly she wanted to run back into his arms, but her pride had already suffered too many hits as it was. "I'll certainly give that some serious consideration. In the meantime, take care, Adan."

"I wish the same to you, Piper."

She chose not to afford Adan another look for fear she might do something foolish, like give him another kiss. But after she climbed into the black limousine a half hour later, she glanced back at the red-stone castle and caught a glimpse of someone standing at the second-floor-terrace railing—the someone who had changed her life.

The sheikh of her dreams. A prince of a guy. The one who got away...with her heart.

Ten

"This arrived for you a little while ago."

Adan turned from the nursery window to find Elena holding a large rectangular box. "More gifts from some sultan attempting to insert themselves in the government with bribes for the baby?"

She crossed the room and handed him the brown-paper-wrapped package. "This one is from the United States. South Carolina, to be exact."

He immediately knew what it contained, though he never believed she would actually honor his request. Not after the way he had regretfully treated her.

While Elena looked on, Adan tore through the wrapping and opened the box to find what appeared to be a painting, exactly as he'd expected. Yet when he pulled it from the box, he didn't expect that the painting would depict a slumbering father holding his sleeping son in remarkable detail, right down to the cleft in his chin and Samuel's prominent left dimple.

"Oh, Adan," Elena began in a reverent voice, "this is such a *bella* gift."

He would wholeheartedly agree, if he could dislodge the annoying lump in his throat. The baby began kicking his legs in rapid-fire succession against the mattress as if he appreciated the gesture.

After resting the painting against the crib, Adan picked up Samuel and held him above his head. "You are quite the noisy character these days."

His son rewarded him with a toothless smile, something he'd begun doing the past month. A milestone that had given him great joy. Bittersweet joy, because Piper had not been around to share in it.

"You should call her and thank her, Adan."

He lowered Samuel to his chest and faced Elena with a frown. "I will send her a handwritten note."

She took the baby from his arms without invitation. "You will do no such thing. She deserves to hear from you personally. She also deserves to know that you have been mourning your loss of her since she departed."

"I have not been mourning," he said, sounding too defensive. "I have been busy raising my son and seeing to my royal duty."

Elena patted his cheek. "You can deceive yourself, but you cannot deceive me. You are so sick with love you could wilt every flower in the palace courtyard with your anxiety."

He avoided her scrutiny by picking up the painting and studying the empty wall above the crib. "I believe this is the perfect spot, right above Samuel's bed so he will go to sleep knowing I am watching over him throughout the night."

"Since it is obvious you are not getting any sleep, why not watch over him in person?"

He returned the painting to the floor at his feet. "I am sleeping fine."

"Ah, yes, and I am entering the marathon in Dubai two weeks from now."

That forced Adan around. "Would you please stop assuming you know everything about me?"

She kissed Samuel's cheek before placing him back in the crib, where he began kicking again at the sight of the colorful mobile above him. "I do know you, *cara*, better than most. When you were Samuel's age, I stayed up many nights while you were teething. When you were a toddler, I put you to bed every night with a book, the reason why you were always such a grand reader. When you were six, and you broke your right arm trying to jump the hedges, I was the one who fed you until you learned to eat with your left hand. And when you were twelve, I discovered those horrid magazines beneath your bed and did not tell your father."

He'd forgotten that incident, with good reason. "I realize you've been there for me through thick and thin, but that does not give you carte blanche to lord over me now that I am an adult."

"I agree, you are an adult."

"I am pleased to know you finally acknowledge that."

"An adult who has absolutely no common sense when it counts most."

He should have expected this as soon as he opened the box. "If you're going to say I made the wrong decision by allowing Piper to leave, I would have to disagree."

"And you would be wrong." Elena leaned back against the crib's railing and donned her stern face. "As I have told both your brothers, you all have a great capacity to love, but it would take a special woman to bring that out in you. Zain and Rafiq learned that lesson by finding that special woman, and so have you. Piper is your soul mate, *cara*. Do not destroy what you could have with her by being so stubborn you cannot see what was right in front of you and you foolishly let go for good."

He hated that she had begun to make sense. "I am not being stubborn. I am being sensible. If you know me as well as you say you do, then you realize I have never stayed involved with one woman longer than six years, and we know how well that turned out."

Elena glared at him much as she had when he'd been a badly behaved boy. "Comparing Talia to Piper is like comparing a cactus to a down comforter. It's true Talia gave you a precious son, but she also gave you continuous grief. Piper gave you not only this touching portrait but also the means to heal your wounds with the truth. And you repay her by not admitting how you feel about her."

"I'm presently not certain how I feel about anything." Other than he resented Elena for pointing out the error in his ways.

"And you, *cara mia,* are guilty of propagating the biggest lie of all if you do not stop denying your love for Piper."

"I have never said I love her." He was too afraid

to leave himself open to that emotion, more so now than ever.

She pointed a finger at his face and glowered at him. "Adan Mehdi, before your obstinate behavior destroys what could be the best thing that has happened to you, listen to me, and listen well. First of all, consider how Piper selflessly cared for your son. How she protected you and Samuel by putting her life on hold while pretending to be your wife, only to be dismissed by you as one would dismiss a servant."

"But I never—"

"Furthermore," she continued without regard for his attempts to halt the tirade, "should you finally regain some semblance of wisdom befitting of royalty and decide to contact her, you will beg her forgiveness for being such a rigid *cretino*."

The woman knew how to deliver a right hook to his ego. "I take offense to my own mother calling me an idiot."

Her expression brightened over the unexpected maternal reference. "It means everything to hear you finally acknowledging me as your mother."

He laid a palm on her cheek. "I suppose I have known that all along. Only a true mother would tolerate my antics."

"And only a true mother would agree to raise a child that is not her own, and love that child's father with all her being despite his shortcomings."

He recognized the reference to Piper, yet he couldn't quell his concerns. "What if I try to contact her and she rejects me? And what do I say to her?"

"You must speak from the heart."

"Something I have never truly mastered."

She sighed. "Adan, your father also viewed revealing emotions as a sign of weakness, and in many ways you have inherited that trait from him. But in reality, it's a brave man who shows vulnerability for the sake of love. I implore you to call on your courage and tell Piper your true feelings, before it is too late."

Admittedly, Elena—his mother—was right. He had never backed away from a battle, and he shouldn't avoid this war to win Piper back. Better still, he had the perfect weapons to convince her to surrender—his well-honed charm, and his remarkable son.

When she sensed movement in the corner of her eye, Piper tore her attention away from the painting of the red-stone palace and brought it to the window that provided natural light. And after she glimpsed the tall man pushing the stroller up the guesthouse walkway, she blinked twice to make sure her imagination hadn't commandeered her vision.

But there he was, the man who'd haunted her dreams for the past four weeks. He wore a crisp tailored black shirt and casual beige slacks, his perfect jaw covered by a shading of whiskers, his slightly ruffled thick dark hair as sexy as ever. And she looked like something the cat had dragged into the garage.

She barely had time to remove the paint-dotted apron and smooth the sides of her lopsided ponytail before the bell chimed. After drawing in a cleansing breath, she opened the door and concealed her shock with a smile. "To what do I owe this honor, Your Highness?"

Adan reached into the stroller and retrieved the baby who had stolen Piper's heart from the moment she'd first held him. "This future pilot insisted on paying a personal visit to the artist who presented us with such a fine painting."

She couldn't believe how cute Sam looked in the miniature flight suit and tiny beige boots. "He really said that, huh?"

"He did."

"Wow. I had no idea three-month-old babies could talk."

"He's an exceptional child."

Born to an exceptionally charming father. A charm he'd clearly passed on to his son, evident when Sam kicked his legs and smiled, revealing his inherited dimples. "Well, don't just stand there, boys. Come inside before you both melt from the heat."

Balancing Sam in one arm, Adan leaned over, retrieved the diaper bag from the basket behind the stroller and slipped the strap over his shoulder. "We are accustomed to the heat, but this humidity is excruciating, so I will gladly accept your offer."

Once he stepped into the foyer, Piper showed him into the small living area and gestured toward the floral sofa. "Have a seat, as soon as you give me the kid."

After he handed Samuel off to her, he claimed the end of the couch and set the bag at his feet. "This is a very comfortable yet quaint abode."

"A nice way of saying *small,*" she said as she sat in the club chair across from him and gently bounced the baby in her lap. "But the rent is cheap. Actually, it's free. My grandparents live in the main house and this is the guest quarters."

"Yes, I know. Your grandfather greeted me as soon as we left the car."

Great. "Not with a shotgun, I hope."

He laughed. "Actually, he wasn't armed. In fact, he was quite cordial. He's still very pleased that he's been granted the water conservation project, and that's going quite well, by the way."

"So I've heard," she said. "I spoke with Rafiq a few days ago."

"He never mentioned that to me."

"He had no reason to mention it, Adan. He's well aware that once I met the terms of our arrangement I'd go back to business as usual."

"And I presume you've done that?"

"Actually, I'm giving a few private art lessons, and I'm looking for a place to open a small gallery. Interestingly enough, my grandfather is willing to invest in the venture."

"How did you convince him to let you leave the company?"

"I told him that it was high time I had a life of my own that included pursuing my personal aspirations. And then I bribed my grandmother into taking up the cause by helping her with a fund-raiser. Between the two of us, he finally caved."

"I'm glad you're happy, Piper," he said, a solemn note to his voice.

She could think of one other thing that would make her happy, but that was only a pipe dream. "I am, for the most part. Are you?"

He rubbed a palm over his jaw. "I'm happy that I have a son and a fulfilling career. Aside from that—"

When Sam began to fuss, Adan withdrew a bottle from the tote, uncapped it and handed to her. "It seems he's getting hungry more often these days. The books

I've read clearly state that an increase in appetite in an infant signals a growth spurt."

"Spoken like the consummate father," Piper said, bringing the return of Adan's smile.

"I am certainly trying my best."

"And you're succeeding," she said as she laid the baby in the crook of her arm and watched as he downed the formula with gusto. "He's definitely grown. Before you know it, he'll be riding a bike. I can't wait to see that." The statement left her mouth before she'd considered how unrealistic she sounded.

"Perhaps he should learn to walk first."

That drew her attention back to Adan. "Yes, you're right. Time is too short to wish it away." After a bout of awkward silence, she added, "How is Elena these days?"

He leaned back against the sofa and draped an arm over the back of the cushions. "She is doing well. We've had several discussions about my father. She insists he was proud of my accomplishments, and claims he had difficulty expressing his emotions. I'm going to endeavor not to do that with Samuel. He deserves to know that his father supports him at every turn."

"And I'm positive you'll manage that just fine."

"You always have had more faith in me than most." He studied her eyes for a long moment. "I didn't realize how much I would miss your company once you left. But I have missed you. Very much."

She had no idea what to say or how to react. She certainly knew better than to hope. "That reminds me. I never saw where you released the statement outlining the reasons behind my departure."

His gaze drifted away. "That is because I never issued that particular statement. We led the press to believe you were on a sabbatical in the States, visiting family."

That made no sense to her at all. "What was the point in delaying the truth? You're eventually going to have to explain why I left and never came back."

Finally, he brought his attention back to her, some unnamed emotion in his eyes. "Perhaps that will not be necessary."

She put the now-empty bottle on the side table and set Sam upright in her lap. "You're hoping that if you sweep it under the rug, everyone will forget I ever existed?"

"I am hoping after you hear what I have to say, you will realize my mission entails alleviating that necessity."

The man insisted on speaking in riddles. "By all means, continue. I'm waiting with bated breath for clarification."

He pushed off the sofa and stood before her. "And I pray I have not waited too long to do this."

As if she'd been thrust in the middle of some surreal dream, Piper watched in awe as Adan fished a black velvet box from his pants pocket and lowered to one knee. She couldn't catch her breath when he opened that box to reveal a massive princess-cut diamond ring. "Piper McAdams, I have never met a woman quite like you, and I have never been in love until you. I probably do not deserve your forgiveness for my careless disregard, but I sincerely believe we both deserve to be together." He tugged the ring from the holder and held it up. "Now, will you do me the honor of being my real wife, and a mother to my son?"

Heaven help her, the cat that had dragged her into

the garage now had hold of her tongue. She could only stare at the glistening diamond, awed by Adan's declaration of love and the knowledge the fairy tale could soon come true. But then came the questions. Should she take this leap of faith? Could she trust that he really wanted her as his wife, not only as a mother for his child? Or was she overanalyzing everything? Then suddenly the baby reached back, grabbed a wayward tendril of hair at her nape and tugged hard, eliciting her involuntary yelp and Adan's scowl.

"That was not the reply I had hoped for," he said gruffly.

She laughed as she extracted Sam's grasp and offered him her pointer finger. "Apparently he was tired of waiting for my answer."

"And I am also growing impatient."

She pulled Sam up from her lap and turned him to face her. "What do you think about this whole thing, little boy? Should I say yes?"

When the baby squealed in response, Adan said, "I do believe he agrees that you should."

She turned Sam around in her lap to face his father and held out her left hand. "I do believe you're right."

After Adan slid the ring into place, he stood and motioned for Piper to join him. Then with baby Sam nestled between them, he kissed her softly and smiled. "I do love you, Piper. More than my MiG-20 jet."

He could be such a cad. A very cute cad. "And I love you more than my purple fluffy slippers that you always found so comical."

His ensuing smile soon disappeared. "On a serious note, as soon as we are wed, I want you to legally become Samuel's mother."

"I would be honored," she said. And she would.

His expression remained overtly somber. "He has a right to know about Talia, although I am at a loss over what to tell him."

"That's simple. When he's old enough to understand, we'll say that his mother loved him enough to give him up because she felt it was the best thing for him. And if I've learned anything at all, I suppose in some way that's what my own mother did for me and Sunny. She wasn't equipped for parenthood."

"But you are," he said. "And I've come to realize that not knowing about Elena did not discount the fact she was always the best mother a man could ask for. She's also a very good grandmother, and she is dying to have you as her daughter-in-law."

Piper couldn't ask for more. "Any idea when we're going to take care of the wedding business?"

"As soon as possible. Perhaps before we return to Bajul."

"We could always hold the ceremony in the family backyard. I provide the groom, and my grandfather provides the shotgun."

Adan laughed as if he didn't have a care in the world. "No need for that. I am a willing participant in establishing a future with you."

And very soon she would no longer be his pretend wife. She would be the real deal.

Epilogue

If a woman wanted to live in a palace, the gorgeous guy standing a few feet away could be just the man to make that come true. And three months ago he had—in a civil ceremony surrounded by her grandparents' lush gardens, sans shotgun. Now Piper McAdams was more than ready to legitimately assume her role as his princess during the elaborate reception held in their honor.

For the past twenty minutes, she'd been schmoozing with wealthy strangers while shamelessly studying her husband's assets. He wore a navy suit adorned with military insignias, a pricey watch on his wrist and a wedding band on his left hand. His usually tousled dark brown hair had been neatly styled for the occasion, but it still complemented the slight shading of whiskers framing his mouth. And those dimples. She'd spotted them the first time she'd laid eyes on him six months ago in the Chicago hotel bar.

And as it had been that night, he was currently speaking to a lithe blonde wearing a chic red sparkling dress, only she didn't see this woman as a threat. In fact, she saw her as simply Madison Foster Mehdi, her sister-in-law and recent addition to Piper's ever-expanding gal-pal club.

Speaking of expanding, a woman dressed in flowing coral chiffon that didn't completely hide a baby bump stood at the ballroom's entrance. She'd come to call her Maysa while most called her queen, and aside from the duties that came along with the title, she served as Sam's stellar doctor and Piper's confidante. The man on her arm, also known as the king, hadn't been as easy to get to know, yet he'd been warming up to his youngest brother's wife, slowly but surely.

All in all, Piper couldn't be happier with her new family. And she couldn't be more pleased when her husband started toward her with that sexy, confident gait that threatened to bring her to her knees.

Once he reached her side, he leaned over and whispered, "I have another gift for you."

"Giving it to me now would be rather inappropriate, don't you think?" she whispered back.

He straightened and smiled. "I'll reserve that gift for later when we are safely ensconced in our room. But this particular present is totally appropriate for the occasion."

Piper took a quick glance at her left hand. "I really think the boulder on my finger is quite sufficient, and so was the wonderful honeymoon in Naples."

"Have you forgotten our time on the beach?"

She faked a frown. "All right, that thing you did to me on the beach was very unforgettable."

"I thought you enjoyed that thing."

She grinned. "I did!"

He pressed a palm against the small of her back and feathered a kiss across her cheek. "Remain here while I retrieve your surprise."

As he headed across the room, Madison came to Piper's side. "Where is he going in such a hurry?"

"He says he has a gift for me."

"Oh, that," Madison replied. "I was beginning to wonder when he was going to get to that."

Piper's eyes went wide. "You know what it is?"

"Yes, I do. In fact, I assisted in acquiring it. And don't look so worried. You'll love it."

Knowing Adan, she probably would. "I'm counting on it."

Madison momentarily scanned the crowd before bringing her attention back to Piper. "I haven't seen Elena yet. She promised she'd come down once she had the babies put to bed."

"She told me she wanted to read them all a book."

"Good luck with that," Madison said, followed by a laugh. "I'm not sure year-old twins and a six-month-old will fit in her lap."

"She enlisted Kira's help," Piper added. "And believe me, Kira is amazing. I'm not sure there's anything she can't do."

"Except hold on to a man," Madison said. "At least according to her."

"A worthless man, maybe. She told me all about her broken engagement. Too bad we snatched up all the Mehdi brothers. She'd make a great sister-in-law."

Madison grinned. "Maybe there's one hiding in

the closet somewhere. Of course, there is their cousin, Rayad, although he's all into the military thing."

Piper still had a lot to learn about the family. "You'd better hope there's not a secret Mehdi hiding out somewhere. That means you'd be in charge of handling that scandal."

"True." Madison pointed at the double doors to her left, where Adan now stood. "Your husband is about to reveal your surprise, so wait and watch and get ready to be wowed."

Piper kept her gaze trained on the doors, wondering what might actually come through them. A new sports car? A pet elephant? Maybe even a...sister?

The minute Sunny caught sight of Piper, she practically ran across the room and engaged her in a voracious hug. And as if they'd been propelled back into the days of their youth, they momentarily jumped up and down until Piper realized exactly where they were and who she now was.

She stopped the girlish celebration, but she couldn't stop her smile. "Sunny McAdams, what are you doing here?"

"Answering your new husband's invitation."

She noticed they'd gained the attention of a room full of dignitaries. "Thanks to our boisterous show of affection, these people are now convinced the new princess is nuttier than a squirrel's nest."

"If the glass slipper fits," Sunny said as she stepped back and surveyed Piper from head to high heels. "You clean up good, sugar plum. Aqua is definitely your color, but I'm clearly underdressed."

Piper smoothed a hand down the bling-embellished satin strapless gown and grinned. "If you'd walked in here wearing something other than black slacks and a white silk blouse, I'd be asking you to return to the mother ship and give me back the real Sunny McAdams."

They shared in a laugh until Adan interrupted the camaraderie. "Did I succeed in surprising you, fair lady?"

She gave him a grateful hug and an enthusiastic kiss. "An excellent surprise, good sir. I do believe you've thought of everything."

"He wanted to make up for me not being at the wedding," Sunny added.

"That's okay, dear sister. You can make it up to me by staying here a few days."

"Unfortunately, I'll be leaving tomorrow. I'm meeting up with Cameron in Africa to cover a few of the most recent uprisings."

Piper hated how her sibling insisted on putting herself in danger, but she was pleased that she seemed to have found her match. "So how's it going with Cameron the cameraman?"

Sunny shrugged. "We're hanging in there. He wants to settle down in suburbia and have a few kids, but I'm not ready for that."

"Take it from me," Madison began, "you can balance career and motherhood. I've managed it with twins."

"And a very accommodating husband." All eyes turned to Zain Mehdi as he slid an arm around his wife's waist. "It's good to see you again, Sunny."

Piper momentarily gaped. "You two have met?"

"Briefly in Nigeria," Sunny said. "But I didn't know who he was until much later, since he was traveling incognito at the time."

Must run in the family, Piper thought when she considered how Adan had concealed his identity. They'd come a long way in a very short time.

As casual conversation continued, Piper noticed a man standing alone a few feet away, his attention focused on the group. "Does anyone know who that man is to my left, holding up the wall?"

"What man?" Adan asked.

"The one who keeps staring."

Sunny glanced over her shoulder before focusing on Piper again. "That's Tarek Azzmar, a corporate investor who hails from Morocco and a billionaire probably ten times over. I met him in Mexico City a few years back when he was opening an orphanage. He's a man of few words and rather reclusive. An enigma wrapped in a mystery, as they say."

"And Rafiq invited him," Zain added. "Apparently he's building a mansion not far from the palace. We'll be able to see his estate when we're standing on the west-facing veranda."

"So much for privacy," Adan muttered. "And with that in mind, if you fine people will excuse us while I have a few moments alone with my wife?"

"By all means," Zain said. "The courtyard outside provides enough protection to begin your honeymoon, if you so choose. My wife will attest to that."

Piper caught a glimpse of Madison elbowing Zain in the side, earning quite a bit of laughter as her husband led her away.

Once in the corner of the deserted vestibule, Adan turned her into his arms. "How does it feel to be an honest-to-goodness princess?"

"Unreal. Surreal. Wonderful."

"I'm glad you are up to the task, and I'm hoping you are willing to take on another."

She suspected she knew where this could be heading. "Hold it right there, hotshot. We have plenty of time to make a sibling for Sam."

"I would like to get to that in the immediate future," he said, "but this task involves your painting skills."

"What would you like me to paint, Your Highness? And please don't tell me one of your planes."

He gave her that earth-shattering, heart-melting grin. "As tempting as that might be, I'm referring to capturing the entire family on canvas. Rafiq, with the council's support, wants to commission you as the official palace artist in order to preserve history."

Piper could think of nothing she would like better. Actually, she could, but she'd take care of that later in bed. "I'm absolutely honored, and I will do my best to prove I'm up to the challenge."

"It is going to be challenging, at that. You'll have to rely on photographs of my father to capture his likeness. And we'll hang that in the foyer."

"I can do that," she said, thankful Adan had thought of it first. "What about your mother?"

"Since she's here for the sitting, that should not be a problem."

Another feat accomplished—his acceptance of Elena. "We'll hang that one in the nursery, next to yours and Sam's."

"And will you be able to paint one of all three of us?"

"Certainly, and I'll make myself look much thinner."

He frowned. "No need for that. You are perfect in every way."

So was he. So was their life, and their love. "Now

that we've taken care of the details, why don't we go up and say good-night to your son?"

"*Our* son."

"You're right. As of this morning, he's legally mine."

He brushed her hair back from her shoulder and kissed her gently. "He has been yours from the beginning, and I will be yours for all time."

In that moment, Piper realized she'd been very lucky to find the sheikh of her dreams. A prince of a guy. The one who got away…and came back, this time to give her his heart.

* * * * *

If you liked THE SHEIKH'S SON,
check out these other sexy sheikhs from
Kristi Gold!
THE RETURN OF THE SHEIKH
ONE NIGHT WITH THE SHEIKH
All available now, from Harlequin Desire!

If you liked this BILLIONAIRES & BABIES *novel,*
watch for the next book in this
#1 bestselling Desire series,
THE NANNY PROPOSITION
by Rachel Bailey,
available August 2014.

COMING NEXT MONTH FROM

HARLEQUIN

Desire

Available August 5, 2014

#2317 THE FIANCÉE CAPER
by Maureen Child
When ex-cop Marie blackmails reformed jewel thief Gianni Coretti into helping her, she expects the sexy Italian to cooperate—not to suggest they go undercover together as bride and groom!

#2318 TAMING THE TAKEOVER TYCOON
Dynasties: The Lassiters • by Robyn Grady
Can good girl Becca Stevens, head of the Lassiters' charitable foundation, keep corporate raider Jack Reed from destroying the family's empire—and win his heart in the bargain?

#2319 THE NANNY PROPOSITION
Billionaires and Babies • by Rachel Bailey
New mom and princess-on-the-run Jenna Peters hides out as a nanny, only to fall for single dad Liam. But will he trust in the passion they've found when her true identity is revealed?

#2320 REDEEMING THE CEO COWBOY
The Slades of Sunset Ranch • by Charlene Sands
Busy raising her infant niece, Susanna is strictly off-limits when her former flame Casey comes back to town. But this rodeo star turned CEO knows no limits...especially when it comes to one very irresistible woman.

#2321 MATCHED TO A PRINCE
Happily Ever After, Inc. • by Kat Cantrell
When a matchmaker pairs Prince Alain with his ex, the scandalous commoner Juliet, he refuses to forgive and forget...and then they're stranded on a deserted island together and old sparks reignite!

#2322 A BRIDE'S TANGLED VOWS
by Dani Wade
Forced to marry for the family business, Aiden Blackstone is surprised by his attraction to his bride. But when someone sabotages his inheritance, can he trust the woman he's let into his bed—and his heart?

YOU CAN FIND MORE INFORMATION ON UPCOMING HARLEQUIN® TITLES, FREE EXCERPTS AND MORE AT WWW.HARLEQUIN.COM.

HDCNM0714

REQUEST YOUR FREE BOOKS!
2 FREE NOVELS PLUS 2 FREE GIFTS!

♦HARLEQUIN®

Desire

ALWAYS POWERFUL, PASSIONATE AND PROVOCATIVE

YES! Please send me 2 FREE Harlequin Desire® novels and my 2 FREE gifts (gifts are worth about $10). After receiving them, if I don't wish to receive any more books, I can return the shipping statement marked "cancel." If I don't cancel, I will receive 6 brand-new novels every month and be billed just $4.55 per book in the U.S. or $4.99 per book in Canada. That's a savings of at least 13% off the cover price! It's quite a bargain! Shipping and handling is just 50¢ per book in the U.S. and 75¢ per book in Canada.* I understand that accepting the 2 free books and gifts places me under no obligation to buy anything. I can always return a shipment and cancel at any time. Even if I never buy another book, the two free books and gifts are mine to keep forever.

225/326 HDN F4ZC

Name	(PLEASE PRINT)
Address	Apt. #
City	State/Prov.	Zip/Postal Code

Signature (if under 18, a parent or guardian must sign)

Mail to the **Harlequin® Reader Service:**
IN U.S.A.: P.O. Box 1867, Buffalo, NY 14240-1867
IN CANADA: P.O. Box 609, Fort Erie, Ontario L2A 5X3

Want to try two free books from another line?
Call 1-800-873-8635 or visit www.ReaderService.com.

* Terms and prices subject to change without notice. Prices do not include applicable taxes. Sales tax applicable in N.Y. Canadian residents will be charged applicable taxes. Offer not valid in Quebec. This offer is limited to one order per household. Not valid for current subscribers to Harlequin Desire books. All orders subject to credit approval. Credit or debit balances in a customer's account(s) may be offset by any other outstanding balance owed by or to the customer. Please allow 4 to 6 weeks for delivery. Offer available while quantities last.

Your Privacy—The Harlequin® Reader Service is committed to protecting your privacy. Our Privacy Policy is available online at www.ReaderService.com or upon request from the Harlequin Reader Service.

We make a portion of our mailing list available to reputable third parties that offer products we believe may interest you. If you prefer that we not exchange your name with third parties, or if you wish to clarify or modify your communication preferences, please visit us at www.ReaderService.com/consumerschoice or write to us at Harlequin Reader Service Preference Service, P.O. Box 9062, Buffalo, NY 14269. Include your complete name and address.

HD13R

Read on for a sneak peek at **Robyn Grady**'s
TAMING THE TAKEOVER TYCOON,
the fifth novel in Harlequin® Desire's
DYNASTIES: THE LASSITERS *series.*
The Lassiter legacy is up for grabs, and this means war....

The Robin Hoods of this world were Becca's heroes. As she watched Jack Reed strike a noble pose, then draw back and release an arrow that hit his target dead center, the irony wasn't lost on her.

Jack Reed was no Robin Hood.

Looking *GQ* hot in jeans and a white button-down, Reed lowered the bow and focused on his guest. The slant of his mouth was so subtle and self-assured, Becca's palm itched to slap the smirk off his face.

He freed the arrow from the target, then sauntered over the manicured lawn to meet her. Although he was expecting her visit, Becca doubted he would welcome what she had to say.

She introduced herself. "Becca Stevens, director of the Lassiter Charitable Foundation." She nodded at the target. "A perfect bull's-eye. Well done."

"I took up archery in college," he said in a voice so deep and darkly honeyed the tone was almost hypnotic. "How may I help you?"

"I'm here to implore you, in J. D. Lassiter's memory, to show some human decency. Walk away from this."

He laughed, a somehow soothing and yet cynical sound. "You don't beat around the bush, do you, Becca?"

No time. "You own a stake in Lassiter Media and rumors are rife. People are bracing for a hostile takeover bid. The charity's donations are down. Regular beneficiaries are actually looking at other options. Want to guess why?"

"I'm sure you'll tell me."

Damn right she would. "The name Jack Reed means trouble. Seriously, how much money does one person need? Is this worth betraying your friend's memory? J.D.'s family?"

"This is not about money. And make no mistake." His uncompromising gaze pierced hers. "I intend to win."

Becca's focus shifted from the steely message in his eyes to the arrow he was holding. Then she thought of this man's lack of empathy—his obsession with personal gain. How could this superb body harbor such a depraved soul? How could Jack Reed live with himself?

Becca took the arrow from his hand, broke the shaft over a knee and, shaking inside, strode away.

Don't miss
TAMING THE TAKEOVER TYCOON by Robyn Grady.

Available August 2014
wherever Harlequin® Desire books and ebooks are sold.

HARLEQUIN®

Desire

ALWAYS POWERFUL, PASSIONATE AND PROVOCATIVE.

**An undercover nanny. A new single father.
Two babies and one scandalous secret!**

Discovering he's a father just rocked scientist Liam Hawke's
world. Hiring Jenna Peters is a stroke of genius. The single
mother of an eight-month-old girl is already working her magic
on his newborn daughter. But how's Liam supposed to ignore
the taboo desire his baby's new nanny is arousing in *him*?

Their employee-boss relationship isn't the only reason Jenna
should keep the billionaire bachelor at arm's length. Once Liam
finds out who she really is, she'll have to say goodbye to the man
she loves *and* their unconventional family. Unless the seductive
single dad makes her a proposition this undercover princess
can't refuse!

Look for

THE NANNY PROPOSITION
BY RACHEL BAILEY

next month from Harlequin Desire.

Look for more dramatic titles from the

BILLIONAIRES AND BABIES

**miniseries, available wherever
books and ebooks are sold!**

HD73332